Mr Roy.
Hill Stre
Crieff

1734. 14-9

THE CHRONICLES OF THE IMP

THE CHRONICLES
OF THE IMP

A ROMANCE

BY
JEFFERY FARNOL

LONDON
SAMPSON LOW, MARSTON & CO., LTD.

MADE AND PRINTED IN GREAT BRITAIN BY
PURNELL AND SONS, LTD., PAULTON (SOMERSET) AND LONDON

CONTENTS

THE
CHRONICLES OF THE IMP

CHAPTER I

TREASURE TROVE

I SAT fishing. I had not caught anything, of course—I rarely do, nor am I fond of fishing in the very smallest degree, but I fished assiduously all the same, because circumstances demanded it.

It had all come about through Lady Warburton, Lisbeth's maternal aunt. Who Lisbeth is you will learn if you trouble to read these veracious narratives—suffice it for the present that she has been an orphan from her youth up, with no living relative save her married sister Julia and her Aunt (with a capital A)—the Lady Warburton aforesaid.

Lady Warburton is small and somewhat bony, with a sharp chin and a sharper nose, and invariably uses a lorgnette; also, she is possessed of much worldly goods.

Precisely a week ago Lady Warburton had requested me to call upon her—had regarded me with a curious exactitude through her lorgnette, and gently though firmly (Lady Warburton is always firm) had suggested that Elizabeth, though a dear child, was young and inclined to be a little self-willed. That she (Lady Warburton) was of opinion that Elizabeth had mistaken the friendship which had existed between us so long for something stronger. That although she (Lady Warburton) quite appreciated the fact that one who wrote books was not necessarily immoral—still I was, of course, a terrible Bohemian, and the air of Bohemia was not calculated to conduce to that degree of matrimonial harmony which she (Lady Warburton) as Elizabeth's Aunt standing to her in place of a mother, could wish for. That, therefore, under these circumstances, my attentions were—etc. etc.

Here I would say in justice to myself that despite the torrent of her eloquence I had at first made some attempt at resistance; but who could hope to contend successfully against a woman possessed of such an indomitable nose and chin, and one, moreover, who could level a jewelled lorgnette with such deadly precision? Still, had Lisbeth been beside me, things might have been different even then; but she had gone away into the country—so Lady Warburton had informed me. Thus, alone and at her mercy, she had succeeded in wringing from me a half promise that I would cease my attentions for the space of six months, "just to give dear Elizabeth time to learn her own heart in regard to the matter."

This was last Monday. On the Wednesday following, as I wandered aimlessly along Piccadilly, at odds with fortune and myself, but especially with myself, my eye encountered the Duchess of Chelsea.

The Duchess is familiarly known as the "Conversational Brook" from the fact that when once she begins she goes on for ever.

Hence, being in my then frame of mind, it was with a feeling of rebellion that I obeyed the summons of her parasol and crossed over to the brougham.

"So she's gone away?" was her greeting as I raised my hat—"Lisbeth," she nodded, "I happened to hear something about her, you know."

It is strange, perhaps, but the Duchess generally does "happen to hear" something about everything.

"And you actually allowed yourself to be bullied into making that promise—Dick! Dick! I'm ashamed of you."

"How was I to help myself?" I began. "You see——"

"Poor boy!" said the Duchess, patting me affectionately with the handle of her parasol, "it wasn't to be expected, of course. You see, I know her—many, many years ago I was at school with Agatha War-burton."

"But she probably didn't use lorgnettes then, and——"

"Her nose was just as sharp though—

'peaky,' I used to call it," nodded the Duchess. "And she has actually sent Lisbeth away—dear child—and to such a horrid quiet little place, too, where she'll have nobody to talk to but that young Selwyn——"

"I beg pardon, Duchess, but——"

"Horace Selwyn, of Selwyn Park—cousin to Lord Selwyn, of Brankesmere. Agatha has been scheming for it a long time, under the rose, you know. Of course, it would be a good match in a way—wealthy, and all that—but I must say he bores me horribly —so very serious and precise!"

"Really!" I exclaimed, "do you mean to say——"

"I expect she will have them married before they know it—Agatha's dreadfully determined. Her character lies in her nose and chin."

"But Lisbeth is not a child—she has a will of her own, and——"

"True," nodded the Duchess, "but is it a match for Agatha's chin? And then, too, it is rather more than possible that you

are become the object of her bitterest scorn
by now."

"But, my dear Duchess——"

"Oh, Agatha is a born diplomat. Of
course she has written before this, and,
without actually saying it, has managed
to convey the fact that you are a monster
of perfidy; and Lisbeth, poor child, who
is probably crying her eyes out, or imagining
she hates you, is ready to accept the first
proposal she receives out of pure pique."

"What on earth can I do?" I exclaimed.

"You might go fishing," the Duchess
suggested thoughtfully.

"Fishing!" I repeated, "—er, to be sure,
but——"

"Riverdale is a very pretty place, they
tell me," pursued the Duchess in the same
thoughtful tone; "there is a house there,
a fine old place, called Fane Court. It
stands facing the river, and adjoins Selwyn
Park, I believe."

"Duchess," I exclaimed, as I jotted down
the address upon my cuff, "I owe you a
debt of gratitude that I can never——"

"Tut, tut!" said her Grace.

"I think I'll start to-day, and——"

"You really couldn't do better," nodded the Duchess.

And so it befell that upon this August afternoon I sat in the shade of the alders fishing, with the smoke of my pipe floating up into the sunshine.

By adroit questioning I had elicited from mine host of the Three Jolly Anglers the precise whereabouts of Fane Court, the abode of Lisbeth's sister, and, guided by his directions, had chosen this sequestered spot, where by simply turning my head I could catch a glimpse of its tall chimneys above the swaying green of tree-tops.

It is a fair thing upon a hot summer's afternoon, within some shady bower, to lie upon one's back and stare up through a network of branches into the limitless blue beyond, while the air is full of the stir of leaves, and the murmur of water among the reeds. Or, propped on lazy elbow, to watch perspiring wretches, short of breath and purple of visage, urge boats up stream or down, each deluding himself into the belief that he is enjoying it. Life under such conditions may seem very fair, as I say; yet I was not happy. The words of the Duchess seemed everywhere about me.

"You are become the object of her bitterest scorn by now," sobbed the wind.

"You are become," etc., etc., moaned the river. It was therefore with no little trepidation that I looked forward to my meeting with Lisbeth.

It was at this moment that the bushes parted and a boy appeared. He was a somewhat diminutive boy, clad in a velvet suit with a lace collar, both of which were plentifully bespattered with mud. He carried his shoes and stockings beneath one arm, and in the other hand swung a hazel branch. He stood with his little brown legs well apart, regarding me with a critical eye; but when at length he spoke his attitude was decidedly friendly.

"Hallo, man!"

"Hallo," I returned; "and who may you be?"

"Well," he answered gravely, "my real name is Reginald Augustus, but they call me 'The Imp.'"

"I can well believe it," I said, eyeing his muddy person.

"If you please, what is an imp?"

"An imp," I explained, "is a sort of an—angel."

"But," he demurred, after a moment's thought, "I haven't got any wings an' things—or a trumpet."

"Your kind never do have wings, or trumpets."

"Oh, I see," he said; and sitting down began to wipe the mud from his legs with his stockings

"Rather muddy, aren't you?" I hinted. The boy cast a furtive glance at his draggled person.

"'Fraid I'm a teeny bit wet, too," he said hesitatingly. "You see, I've been playing at 'Romans,' an' I had to wade, you know, 'cause I was the standard-bearer who jumped

into the sea waving his sword an' crying
'Follow me!' You remember him, don't
you?—he's in the history book."

"To be sure," I nodded; "a truly heroic
character. But if you were the Romans,
where were the Ancient Britons?"

"Oh, they were the reeds, you know;
you ought to have seen me slay them. It
was fine; they went down like—like——"

"Corn before the sickle," I suggested.

"Yes, just!" he cried; "the battle raged
for hours."

"You must be rather tired."

"'Course not," he answered, with an indignant look. "I'm not a girl—an' I'm
nearly nine, too."

"I gather from your tone that you are
not partial to the sex—you don't like girls,
eh, Imp?"

"Should think not," he returned; "silly
things, girls are. There's Dorothy, you
know; we were playing at executions the
other day—she was Mary Queen of Scots
an' I was the headsman. I made a lovely
axe with wood and silver paper, you know;

an' when I cut her head off she cried awfully, an' I only gave her the weeniest little tap— an' they sent me to bed at six o'clock for it. I believe she cried on purpose—awfully caddish, wasn't it?"

"My dear Imp," said I, "the older you grow the more the depravity of the sex will become apparent to you."

"Do you know, I like you," he said, regarding me thoughtfully. "I think you are fine."

"Now that's very nice of you, Imp; in common with my kind I have a weakness for flattery—please go on."

"I mean, I think you are jolly."

"As to that," I said, shaking my head and sighing, "appearances are often very deceptive; at the heart of many a fair blossom there is a canker-worm."

"I'm awfull' fond of worms, too," said the Imp.

"Indeed?"

"Yes. I got a pocketful yesterday, only Auntie found out an' made me let them all go again."

"Ah—yes," I said sympathetically; "that was the woman of it."

"I've only got one left now," continued the Imp; and thrusting a hand into the pocket of his knickerbockers he drew forth six inches or so of slimy worm and held it out to me upon his small, grimy palm.

"He's nice and fat!" I said.

"Yes," nodded the Imp; "I caught him under the gooseberry bushes;" and dropping it back into his pocket he proceeded to don his shoes and stockings.

"'Fraid I'm a bit muddy," he said suddenly.

"Oh, you might be worse," I answered reassuringly.

"Do you think they'll notice it?" he inquired contorting himself horribly in order to view the small of his back.

"Well," I hesitated, "it all depends, you know."

"I don't mind Dorothy, or Betty the cook, or the governess—it's Auntie Lisbeth I'm thinking about."

"Auntie—who?" I exclaimed, regardless of grammar.

"Auntie Lisbeth," repeated the Imp.

"What is she like?"

"Oh, she's grown up big, only she's nice. She came to take care of Dorothy an' me while mother goes away to get nice an' strong—oh, Auntie Lisbeth's jolly, you know."

"With black hair and blue eyes?" The Imp nodded.

"And a dimple at the corner of her mouth?" I went on dreamily.

"An' do you know my Auntie Lisbeth?"

"I think it extremely probable—in fact, I'm sure of it."

"Then you might lend me your handkerchief, please; I tied mine to a bush for a flag, you know, an' it blew away."

"You'd better come here and I'll give you a rub down, my Imp." He obeyed, with many profuse expressions of gratitude.

"Have you got any Aunties?" he inquired, as I laboured upon his miry person.

"No," I answered, shaking my head;

"unfortunately mine are all Aunts, and that is vastly different."

"Oh," said the Imp, regarding me with a puzzled expression; "are they nice—I mean do they ever read to you out of the history book, an' help you to sail boats, an' paddle?"

"Paddle?" I repeated.

"Yes. My Aunt Lisbeth does. The other day we got up awfull' early an' went for a walk, an' we came to the river, so we took off our shoes an' stockings an' we paddled; it was ever so jolly, you know. An' when Auntie wasn't looking I found a frog an' put it in her stocking."

"Highly strategic, my Imp! Well?"

"It was awfull' funny," he said, smiling dreamily. "When she went to put 'em on she gave a little high-up scream, like Dorothy does when I pinch her a bit—an' then she throwed them both away, 'cause she was afraid there was frogs in both of them. Then she put on her shoes without any stockings at all, so I hid them."

"Where?" I cried eagerly.

"Reggie!" called a voice some distance away—a voice I recognised with a thrill. "Reggie!"

"Imp, would you like half a crown?"

"'Course I would; but you might clean my back, please!" and he began rubbing himself feverishly with his cap, after the fashion of a scrubbing brush.

"Look here," I said, pulling out the coin, "tell me where you hid them—quick—and I'll give you this." The Imp held out his hand, but, even as he did so, the bushes parted, and Lisbeth stood before us. She gave a little low cry of surprise at sight of me, and then frowned.

"You?" she exclaimed.

"Yes," I answered, raising my cap. And there I stopped, trying frantically to remember the speech I had so carefully prepared —the greeting which was to have explained my conduct and disarmed her resentment at the very outset. But, rack my brain as I would, I could think of nothing but the reproach in her eyes—her disdainful mouth and chin—and that one haunting phrase—

"'I suppose I am become the object of your bitterest scorn by now?'" I found myself saying.

"My Aunt informed me of—of everything, and naturally——"

"Let me explain," I began.

"Really, it is not at all necessary."

"But, Lisbeth, I must—I insist——"

"Reginald," she said, turning toward the Imp, who was still busy with his cap, "it's nearly tea-time, and—why, whatever have you been doing to yourself?"

"For the last half-hour." I interposed, "we have been exchanging our opinions on the sex."

"An' talking 'bout worms," added the Imp. "This man is fond of worms, too, Auntie Lisbeth—I like him."

"Thanks," I said; "but let me beg of you to drop your very distant mode of address. Call me Uncle Dick."

"But you're not my Uncle Dick, you know," he demurred.

"Not yet, perhaps; but there's no knowing what may happen some day if your Auntie

thinks us worthy—so take time by the
forelock, my Imp, and call me Uncle Dick."

Whatever Lisbeth might or might not
have said was checked by the patter of
footsteps, and a little girl tripped into view,
with a small, fluffy kitten cuddled in her
arms.

"Oh, Auntie Lisbeth," she began, but
stopped to stare at me over the back of the
fluffy kitten.

"Hallo, Dorothy!" cried the Imp; "this
is Uncle Dick. You can come an' shake
hands with him if you like."

"I didn't know I had an Uncle Dick,"
said Dorothy, hesitating.

"Oh yes; it's all right," answered the
Imp reassuringly. "I found him, you know,
an' he likes worms, too!"

Dorothy gave me her hand demurely.

"How do you do, Uncle Dick?" she said
in a quaint old-fashioned way. "Reginald
is always finding things, you know, an' he
likes worms, too!"

From somewhere near by there came the
silvery chime of a bell.

"Why, there's the tea-bell!" exclaimed Lisbeth; "and, Reginald, you have to change those muddy clothes. Say good-bye to Mr. Brent, children, and come along."

"Imp," I whispered, as the others turned away, "where did you hide those stockings?" And I slipped the half-crown into his ready palm.

"Along the river there's a tree—very big an' awfull' fat, you know, with a lot of stickie-out branches, an' a hole in its stomach —they're in there.

"Reginald!" called Lisbeth.

"Up stream or down?"

"That way," he answered, pointing vaguely down stream; and with a nod that brought the yellow curls over his eyes he scampered off.

"Along the river," I repeated, "in a big, fat tree with a lot of stickie-out branches!" It sounded a trifle indefinite, I thought— still I could but try. So having packed up my rod I set out upon the search.

It was strange, perhaps, but nearly every tree I saw seemed to be either "big" or "fat"—and all of them had "stickie-out" branches.

Thus the sun was already low in the west, and I was lighting my fifth pipe when I at length observed the tree in question.

A great pollard oak it was, standing upon the very edge of the stream, easily distinguishable by its unusual size and the fact that at some time or another it had been riven by lightning. After all, the Imp's description had been in the main correct; it was "fat," immensely fat; and I hurried joyfully forward.

I was still some way off when I saw the distinct flutter of a white skirt, and—yes, sure enough, there was Lisbeth, walking quickly, too, and she was a great deal nearer the tree than I.

Prompted by a sudden conviction I dropped my rod and began to run. Immediately Lisbeth began running too. I threw away my creel and sprinted for all I was worth. I had earned some small fame at this sort of thing in my university days, yet I arrived at the tree with only a very few yards to

spare. Throwing myself upon my knees,
I commenced a feverish search, and presently
—more by good fortune than anything else—
my random fingers encountered a soft silken
bundle. When Lisbeth came up, flushed and
panting, I held them in my hands.

"Give them to me!" she cried.

"I'm sorry——"

"Please," she begged.

"I'm very sorry——"

"Mr. Brent," said Lisbeth, drawing
herself up, "I'll trouble you for my—
them."

"Pardon me, Lisbeth," I answered, "but
if I remember anything of the law of 'treasure-
trove' one of these should go to the Crown,
and one belongs to me."

Lisbeth grew quite angry—one of her
few bad traits.

"You will give them up at once—immediately."

"On the contrary," I said very gently,
"seeing the Crown can have no use for one,
I shall keep them both to dream over when
the nights are long and lonely!"

Lisbeth actually stamped her foot at me, and I tucked "them" into my pocket.

"How did you know they—they were here?" she enquired after a pause.

"I was directed to a tree with 'stickie-out' branches," I answered.

"Oh, that Imp!" she exclaimed, and stamped her foot again.

"Do you know, I've grown quite attached to that nephew of mine already?" I said.

"He's not a nephew of yours," cried Lisbeth quite hotly.

"Not legally, perhaps; that is where you might be of such assistance to us, Lisbeth. A boy with only an aunt here and there, is unbalanced, so to speak; he requires the stronger influence of an uncle. Not," I continued hastily, "that I would depreciate aunts—by the way, he has but one, I believe?" Lisbeth nodded coldly.

"Of course," I nodded, "and very lucky in that one—extremely fortunate. Now, years ago, when I was a boy, I had three, and all of them blanks, so to speak. I mean none of them ever dare to me out of the history book, or helped me to sail boats, or paddled and lost their—— No, mine used to lecture me about my hair and nails, I remember, and glare at me over the big tea-urn until I choked into my tea-cup. A truly desolate childhood mine. I had no big-fisted uncle to thump me persuasively when I needed it; had fortune granted me one I might have been a very different man, Lisbeth. You behold in me a horrible example of what one may become whose boyhood has been denuded of uncles."

"If you will be so very obliging as to return my—my property."

"My dear Lisbeth," I sighed, "be reasonable; suppose we talk of something else"— and I attempted, though quite vainly, to direct her attention to the glories of the sunset.

A fallen tree lay near by, upon which Lisbeth seated herself with a certain determined set of her little round chin that I knew well.

"And how long do you intend keeping me here?" she asked in a resigned tone.

"Always, if I had my way."

"Really?" she said, and whole volumes could never describe all the scorn she managed to put into that single word. "You see," she continued, "after what Aunt Agatha wrote and told me——"

"Lisbeth," I broke in, "if you'll only——"

"I naturally supposed——"

"If you'll only let me explain——"

"That you would abide by the promise you made her and wait——"

"Until you knew your own heart," I put in. "The question is how long will it take you? Probably, if you would allow me to teach you——"

"Your presence here now stamps you as—as horribly deceitful!"

"Undoubtedly," I nodded; "but, you see, when I was foolish enough to give that promise, your very excellent Aunt made no reference to her intentions regarding a certain Mr. Selwyn."

"Oh!" exclaimed Lisbeth. And feeling that I had made a point, I continued with redoubled ardour:

"She gave me to understand that she merely wished you to have time to know your own heart in the matter. Now, as I said before, how long will it take you to find out, Lisbeth?"

She sat, chin in hand, staring straight before her, and her black brows were still drawn together in a frown. But I watched her mouth—just where the scarlet underlip curved up to meet its fellow.

Lisbeth's mouth is a trifle wide, perhaps, and rather full-lipped, and somewhere at one corner—I can never be quite certain of its exact location, because its appearance is, as a rule, so very meteoric—but somewhere there is a dimple. Now, if ever there was an arrant traitor in this world it is that dimple; for let her expression be ever so guileless, let her wistful eyes be raised with a look of tears in their blue depths, despite herself that dimple will spring into life and undo it all in a moment. So it was now; even as I watched, it quivered round her lips, and feeling herself betrayed, the frown vanished altogether and she smiled.

"And now, Dick, suppose you give me my—my——"

"Conditionally," I said, sitting down beside her.

The sun had set, and from somewhere among the purple shadows of the wood the rich, deep notes of a blackbird came to us, with pauses now and then, filled in with the rustle of leaves and the distant lowing of cows.

"Not far from the village of Down in Kent," I began dreamily, "there stands an old house with quaint, high-gabled roofs and twisted Tudor chimneys. Many years ago it was the home of fair ladies and gallant gentlemen, but its glory is long past. And yet, Lisbeth, when I think of it at such an hour as this, and with you beside me, I begin to wonder if we could not manage between us to bring back the old order of things."

Lisbeth was silent.

"It has a wonderful old-fashioned rose garden, and you are fond of roses, Lisbeth."

"Yes," she murmured; "I'm very fond of roses."

"They would be in full bloom now," I suggested.

There was another pause, during which the blackbird performed three or four difficult arias with astonishing ease and precision.

"Aunt Agatha is fond of roses, too!" said Lisbeth at last very gravely. "Poor dear Aunt, I wonder what she would say if she could see us now?"

"Such things are better left to the imagination," I answered.

"I ought to write and tell her," murmured Lisbeth.

"But you won't do that, of course?"

"No, I won't do that, if——"

"Well?"

"If you will give me—them."

"One," I demurred.

"Both!"

"On one condition, then—just once, Lisbeth?"

Her lips were very near, her lashes drooped,

and for one delicious moment she hesitated. Then I felt a little tug at my coat pocket, and springing to her feet she was away with "them" clutched in her hand.

"Trickery!" I cried, and started in pursuit.

There is a path through the woods leading to the Shrubbery at Fane Court. Down this she fled, and her laughter came to me on the wind. I was close upon her when she reached the gate, and darting through turned, flushed but triumphant.

"I've won!" she mocked, nodding her head at me.

"Who can cope with the duplicity of a woman?" I retorted. "But, Lisbeth, you will give me one—just one?"

"It would spoil the pair."

"Oh, very well," I sighed, "good-night, Lisbeth," and lifting my cap I turned away.

There came a ripple of laughter behind me, something struck me softly upon the cheek, and, stooping, I picked up that which lay half unrolled at my feet, but when I looked round Lisbeth was gone.

B

So presently I thrust "them" into my pocket and walked back slowly along the river path toward the hospitable shelter of the Three Jolly Anglers.

CHAPTER II

THE SHERIFF OF NOTTINGHAM

To sit beside a river on a golden afternoon listening to its whispered melody, while the air about one is fragrant with summer, and heavy with the drone of unseen wings! —What ordinary mortal could wish for more?

And yet, though conscious of this fair world about me, I was still uncontent, for my world was incomplete—nay, lacked its most essential charm, and I sat with my ears on the stretch, waiting for Lisbeth's chance footstep on the path and the soft whisper of her skirts.

The French are indeed a great people, for among many other things they alone have caught that magic sound a woman's garments make as she walks, and given it to the world in the one word "*frou-frou.*"

O wondrous word! O word sublime! How full art thou of delicate suggestion! Truly there can be no sweeter sound to ears masculine upon a golden summer afternoon—or any other time, for that matter—than the soft "*frou-frou*" that tells him *She is coming.*

At this point my thoughts were interrupted by something which hurtled through the air and splashed into the water at my feet. Glancing at this object, I recognised the loud-toned cricket cap affected by the Imp, and reaching for it, I fished it out on the end of my rod. It was a hideous thing of red, white, blue, and green—a really horrible affair, and therefore much prized by its owner, as I knew.

Behind me the bank rose some four or five feet, crowned with willows and underbrush, from the other side of which there now came a prodigious rustling and panting. Rising to my feet, therefore, I parted the leaves with extreme care, and beheld the Imp himself.

He was armed to the teeth—that is to say, a wooden sword swung at his thigh, a tin bugle depended from his belt, and he carried a bow and arrow. Opposite him was another boy, particularly ragged at knee and elbow, who stood with hands thrust into his pockets and grinned.

"Base caitiff, hold!" cried the Imp, fitting an arrow to the string; "stand an' deliver. Give me my cap, thou varlet, thou!" The boy's grin expanded.

"Give me my cap, base slave, or I'll shoot you—by my troth!" As he spoke the Imp aimed his arrow, whereupon the boy ducked promptly.

"I ain't got yer cap," he grinned from the shelter of his arm. "It's been an' gone an' throwed itself into the river!" The Imp let fly his arrow, which was answered by a yell from the Base Varlet.

"Yah!" he cried derisively as the Imp drew his sword with a melodramatic flourish. "Yah! put down that stick an' I'll fight yer."

The Imp indignantly repudiated his trusty weapon being called "a stick"—"an' J don't think," he went on, "that Robin Hood ever fought without his sword. Let's see what the book says," and he drew a very crumpled paper-covered volume from his pocket, which he consulted with knitted brows, while the Base Varlet watched him, open-mouthed.

"Oh, yes," nodded the Imp; "it's all right. Listen to this!" and he read as follows in a stern, deep voice:

"'Then Robin tossed aside his trusty blade, an' laying bare his knotted arm, approached the dastardly ruffian with many a merry quip and jest, prepared for the fierce death-grip.'"

Hereupon the Imp laid aside his book and weapons and proceeded to roll up his sleeve, having done which to his satisfaction, he faced round upon the Base Varlet.

"Have at ye, dastardly ruffian!" he cried, and therewith ensued a battle, fierce and fell.

If his antagonist had it in height, the Imp made up for it in weight—he is a particularly solid Imp—and thus the struggle lasted for some five minutes without any appreciable advantage to either, when, in eluding one of the enemy's desperate rushes, the Imp stumbled, lost his balance, and next moment I had caught him in my arms. For a space "the enemy" remained panting on the bank above, and then with another yell turned and darted off among the bushes.

"Hallo, Imp!" I said.

"Hallo, Uncle Dick!" he returned.

"Hurt?" I enquired.

"Wounded a bit in the nose, you know," he answered, mopping that organ with his handkerchief; "but did you see me punch 'yon varlet' in the eye?"

"Did you, Imp?"

"I think so, Uncle Dick; only I do wish I'd made him surrender. The book says that Robin Hood always made his enemies 'surrender an' beg their life on trembling knee!' Oh, it must be fine to see your enemies on their knee!"

"Especially if they tremble," I added.

"Do you s'pose that boy—I mean 'yon base varlet' would have surrendered?"

"Not a doubt of it—if he hadn't happened to push you over the bank first."

"Oh!" murmured the Imp rather dubiously.

"By the way," I said, "where is your Auntie Lisbeth?"

"Well, I chased her up the big apple-tree with my bow an' arrow."

"Of course," I nodded. "Very right and proper!"

"You see," he explained, "I wanted her to be a wild elephant an' she wouldn't."

"Extremely disobliging of her!"

"Yes, wasn't it? So when she was right up I took away the ladder an' hid it."

"Highly strategic, my Imp."

"So then I turned into Robin Hood. I hung my cap on a bush to shoot at, you know, an' 'the Base Varlet' came up an' ran off with it."

"And there it is," I said, pointing to where it lay. The Imp received it with profuse thanks, and, having wrung out the water, clapped it upon his curls and sat down beside me.

"I found another man who wants to be my uncle," he began.

"Oh, indeed?"

"Yes; but I don't want any more, you know."

"Of course not. One like me suffices for your everyday needs—eh, my Imp?"

The Imp nodded. "It was yesterday," he continued. "He came to see Auntie Lisbeth, an' I found them in the summer-house in the orchard. An' I heard him say, 'Miss Elizabeth, you're prettier than ever!'"

"Did he though, confound him!"

"Yes, an' then Auntie Lisbeth looked silly, an' then he saw me behind a tree an' he looked silly, too. Then he said, 'Come here, little man!' An' I went, you know, though I do hate to be called 'little man.' Then he said he'd give me a shilling if I'd call him Uncle Frank."

"And what did you answer?"

"'Fraid I'm awfull' wicked," sighed the Imp, shaking his head, "'cause I told him a story."

"Did you, Imp?"

"Yes. I said I didn't want his shilling, an' I do, you know, most awfully, to buy a spring-pistol with."

"Oh, well, we'll see what can be done about the spring-pistol," I answered. "And so you don't like him, eh?"

"Should think not," returned the Imp promptly. "He's always so—so awfull' clean, an' wears a little moustache with teeny sharp points on it."

"Anyone who does that deserves all he gets," I said, shaking my head. "And what is his name?"

"The Honourable Frank Selwyn, an' he lives at Selwyn Park—the next house to ours."

"Oho!" I exclaimed, and whistled.

"Uncle Dick," said the Imp, breaking in upon a somewhat unpleasant train of thought conjured up by this intelligence, "will you come an' be 'Little-John under the merry greenwood tree'? Do."

"Why, what do you know about 'the merry greenwood,' Imp?"

"Oh, lots!" he answered, hastily pulling out the tattered book. "This is all about Robin Hood an' Little-John. Ben, the gardener's boy, lent it to me. Robin Hood was a fine chap, an' so was Little-John, an' they used to set ambushes an' capture the Sheriff of Nottingham an' all sorts of caddish barons, an' tie them to trees."

"My Imp," I said, shaking my head, "the times are sadly changed. One cannot tie barons—caddish or otherwise—to trees in these degenerate days."

"No, I s'pose not," sighed the Imp dolefully; "but I do wish you would be Little-John, Uncle Dick."

"Oh, certainly, Imp, if it will make you any happier; though of a truth, bold Robin," I continued after the manner of the story-books, "Little-John hath a mind to bide awhile and commune with himself here; yet give but one blast upon thy bugle horn and thou shalt find my arm and quarter-staff ready and willing enough, I'll warrant you!"

"That sounds awfull' fine, Uncle Dick, only—you haven't got a quarter-staff, you know."

"Yea, 'tis here!" I answered, and detached the lower joint of my fishing-rod. The Imp rose, and folding his arms, surveyed me as Robin Hood himself might have done—that is to say, with an "eye of fire."

"So be it, my faithful Little-John," quoth he; "meet me at the Blasted Oak at midnight. An' if I shout for help—I mean blow my bugle—you'll come an' rescue me, won't you, Uncle Dick?"

"Ay; trust me for that," I answered, all unsuspecting.

"'Tis well!" nodded the Imp; and with a wave of his hand he turned and scrambling up the bank, disappeared.

Of the existence of Mr. Selwyn I was already aware, having been notified in this particular by the Duchess, as I have told in the foregoing narrative.

Now, a rival in air—in the abstract, so to

speak—is one thing, but a rival who was on a sufficiently intimate footing to deal in personal compliments, and above all, one who was already approved of and encouraged by the powers that be, in the person of Lady Warburton—Lisbeth's formidable aunt —was another consideration altogether.

"Miss Elizabeth, you're prettier than ever!"

Somehow the expression rankled.

What right had he to tell her such things?—and in a summer-house, too;—the insufferable audacity of the fellow!

A pipe being indispensable to the occasion, I took out my matchbox, only to find that it contained but a solitary vesta.

The afternoon had been hot and still hitherto, with never so much as a breath of wind stirring; but no sooner did I prepare to strike that match than from somewhere there came a sudden flaw of wind that ruffled the glassy waters of the river and set every leaf whispering. Waiting until what I took to be a favourable opportunity, with infinite precaution I struck a light.

It flickered in a sickly fashion for a moment between my sheltering palms, and immediately expired.

This is but one example of that "Spirit of the Perverse" pervading all things mundane which we poor mortals are called upon to bear as best we may. Therefore I tossed aside the charred match, and, having searched fruitlessly through my pockets for another, waited philosophically for some "good Samaritan" to come along. The bank I have mentioned sloped away gently on my left, thus affording an uninterrupted view of the path.

Now as my eyes followed this winding path I beheld an individual some distance away who crawled upon his hands and knees, evidently searching for something. As I watched, he succeeded in raking a Panama hat from beneath a bush, and, having dusted it carefully with his handkerchief replaced it upon his head and continued his advance.

With some faint hope that there might be a loose match hiding away in some corner of my pockets, I went through them again more carefully, but alas! with no better success; whereupon I gave it up and turned to glance at the approaching figure.

My astonishment may be readily imagined when I beheld him in precisely the same attitude as before—that is to say, upon his hands and knees.

I was yet puzzling over this phenomenon when he again raked out the Panama on the end of the hunting-crop he carried, dusted it as before, looking about him the while with a bewildered air, and, setting it firmly upon his head, came down the path.

He was a tall young fellow, scrupulously neat and well groomed from the polish of his brown riding-boots to his small, sleek moustache, which was parted with elaborate care and twisted into two fine points. There was about his whole person an indefinable air of self-complacent satisfaction, but he carried his personality in his moustache, so to speak, which, though small, as I say, and precise to a hair, yet obtruded itself upon one in a vaguely unpleasant way. Noticing all this, I thought I might make a very good guess as to his identity if need were.

All at once, as I watched him—like a bird rising from her nest—the devoted Panama rose in the air, turned over once or twice and fluttered (I use the word figuratively) into a bramble bush. Bad language was writ large in every line of his body as he stood looking about him, the hunting-crop quivering in his grasp.

It was at this precise juncture that his eye encountered me, and, pausing only to recover his unfortunate headgear, he strode toward where I sat.

"Do you know anything about this?" he inquired in a somewhat aggressive manner, holding up a length of black thread.

"A piece of ordinary pack-thread," I answered affecting to examine it with a critical eye.

"Do you know anything about it?"

he said again, evidently in a very bad temper.

"Sir," I answered, "I do not."

"Because if I thought you did——"

"Sir," I broke in, "you'll excuse me, but that seems a very remarkable hat of yours."

"I repeat, if I thought you did——"

"Of course," I went on, "each to his taste, but personally I prefer one with less 'gymnastic' and more 'stay-at-home' qualities."

The hunting-crop was raised threateningly.

"Mr. Selwyn?" I inquired in a conversational tone.

The hunting-crop hesitated and was lowered.

"Well, sir?"

"Ah, I thought so," I said, bowing; "permit me to trespass upon your generosity to the extent of a match—or, say, a couple."

Mr. Selwyn remained staring down at me for a moment, and I saw the points of his moustache positively curling with indignation. Then without deigning a reply, he turned on his heel and strode away. He had not gone more than thirty or forty paces, however, when I heard him stop and mutter savagely—I did not need to look to learn the reason—I admit I chuckled. But my merriment was short-lived, for a moment later came the feeble squeak of a horn followed by a shout and the Imp's voice upraised in dire distress.

"Little-John! Little-John! to the rescue!" it called.

I hesitated, for I will freely confess that when I had made that promise to the Imp it was with small expectation that I should be called upon to fulfil it. Still, a promise is a promise; so I sighed, and picking up the joint of my fishing-rod, clambered up the bank. Glancing in the direction of the cries, I beheld Robin Hood struggling in the foe's indignant grasp.

Now, there were but two methods of procedure open to me as I could see—the serious or the frankly grotesque. Naturally

I chose the latter, and, quarter-staff on shoulder, I swaggered down the path with an air that Little-John himself might well have envied.

"Beshrew me!" I cried, confronting the amazed Mr. Selwyn. "Who dares lay hands on bold Robin Hood? Away, base rogue, hie thee hence, or I am like to fetch thee a dour ding on that pate o' thine!"

Mr. Selwyn loosed the Imp and stared at me in speechless amazement, as well he might.

"Look ye, master," I continued, entering into the spirit of the thing, "no man lays hand on Robin Hood whiles Little-John can twirl a staff or draw a bow-string—no!"

The Imp, retired to a safe distance, stood hearkening in a transport till, bethinking him of his part, he fished out the tattered book and began surreptitiously turning over the pages; as for Mr. Selwyn, he only fumbled at his moustache and stared.

"Aye, but I know thee," I went on again; "by thy sly and crafty look, by thy scalloped cape and chain of office, I know thee for that same Sheriff of Nottingham that hath sworn to our undoing. Go to! didst think to take Robin—in the greenwood? Out upon thee! Thy years should have taught thee better wisdom. Out upon thee!"

"Now will I feed"—began the Imp, with the book carefully held behind him—"now will I feed fat mine vengeance—to thy knees for a scurvy rascal!"

"Aye," I nodded, "'twere well he should do penance on his marrow-bones from hither to Nottingham Town; but as thou art strong—be merciful, Robin."

Mr. Selwyn still curled the point of his moustache.

"Are you mad," he enquired, "or only drunk?"

"As to that, good master Sheriff, it doth concern thee nothing—but mark you! 'tis an ill thing to venture within the greenwood whiles Robin Hood and Little-John be abroad."

Mr. Selwyn shrugged his shoulders and turned to the Imp.

"I am on my way to see your Aunt Elizabeth, and shall make it my particular care to inform her of your conduct, and see that you are properly punished. As for you, sir," he continued, addressing me, "I shall inform the police that there is a madman at large."

At this double-barrelled threat the Imp was plainly much dismayed, and coming up beside me, slipped his hand into mine, and I promptly pocketed it.

"Sweet master Sheriff," I said, sweeping off my cap in true outlaw fashion, "the way is long and something lonely; methinks —we will therefore e'en accompany you, and may perchance lighten the tedium with quip and quirk and a merry stave or so."

Seeing the angry rejoinder upon Mr. Selwyn's lips, I burst forth incontinent into the following ditty, the words extemporised to the tune of "Bonnie Dundee":

> " There lived a sheriff in Nottinghamshire,
>   With a hey derry down and a down:
>   He was fond of good beef, but was fonder of beer,
>   With a hey derry down and a down."

By the time we reached the Shrubbery gate the Imp was in an ecstasy, and Mr. Selwyn once more reduced to speechless indignation and astonishment. Here our ways diverged, Mr. Selwyn turning toward the house, while the Imp and I made our way to the orchard at the rear.

"Uncle Dick," he said, halting suddenly, "do you think he will tell—really?"

"My dear Imp," I answered, "a man who wears 'points on his moustache' is capable of anything."

"Then I shall be sent to bed for it, I know I shall!"

"To run into a thread tied across the path must have been very annoying," I said, shaking my head thoughtfully, "especially with a brand-new hat!"

"They were only 'ambushes,' you know, Uncle Dick."

"To be sure," I nodded. "Now, observe, my Imp, here is a shilling; go and buy that spring-pistol you were speaking of, and take your time about it; I'll see what can be done in the meanwhile."

The Imp was reduced to incoherent thanks.

"That's all right," I said, "but you had better hurry off."

He obeyed with alacrity, disappearing in the direction of the village, while I went on towards the orchard to find Lisbeth. And presently, sure enough, I did find her—that is to say, part of her, for the foliage of that particular tree happened to be very thick, and I could see nothing of her but a foot.

A small and shapely foot it was that swung audaciously to and fro; a foot in a ridiculously out-of-place little patent-leather shoe.

I approached softly, with the soul of me in my eyes, so to speak, yet, despite my caution, she seemed to become aware of my presence in some way—the foot faltered in its swing and vanished as the leaves were parted, and Lisbeth looked down at me.

"Oh, it's you?" she said, and I fancied. she seemed quite pleased. "You'll find a step-ladder somewhere about—it can't be very far."

"Thanks," I answered, "but I don't want one."

"No; but I do; I want to get down. That little wretched Imp hid the ladder, and I've been here all the afternoon," she wailed.

"But then you refused to be an elephant you know," I reminded her.

"He shall go to bed for it—directly after tea!" she said.

"Lisbeth," I returned, "I firmly believe your nature to be altogether too sweet and forgiving——"

"I want to come down!"

"Certainly," I said; "put your left foot in my right hand, take firm hold of the branch above, and let yourself sink gently into my arms."

"Oh!" she exclaimed suddenly, "here's Mr. Selwyn coming," and following her glance, I saw a distinct Panama approaching.

"Lisbeth," said I, "are you anxious to see him?"

"In this ridiculous situation—of course not!"

"Very well then, hide—just sit there and leave matters to me and——".

"Hush," she whispered, and at that moment Selwyn emerged into full view. Catching sight of me, he stopped in evident surprise.

"I was told I should find Miss Elizabeth here," he said stiffly.

"It would almost appear that you had been misinformed," I answered. For a moment he seemed undecided what to do. Would he go away? I wondered. Evidently not, for after glancing about him he sat himself down upon a rustic seat near by with a certain resolute air that I did not like. I must get rid of him at all hazards.

"Sir," said I, "can I trespass on your generosity to the extent of a match—or say a couple?" After a brief hesitation he drew out a very neat silver match-box, which he handed to me.

"A fine day, sir?" I said, puffing at my pipe.

Mr. Selwyn made no reply.

"I hear that the crops are looking particularly healthy this year," I went on.

Mr. Selwyn appeared to be utterly lost in the contemplation of an adjacent tree.

"To my mind an old apple-tree is singularly picturesque," I began again. "Nice nobbly branches, don't you know?"

Mr. Selwyn began to fidget.

"And then," I pursued, "they tell me that apples are so good for the blood."

Mr. Selwyn shifted his gaze to the toe of his riding-boot, and for a space there was silence, so much so, indeed, that an inquisitive rabbit crept up and sat down to watch us with much interest, until—evidently remembering some pressing engagement— he disappeared with a flash of his white tail.

"Talking of rabbits," said I, "they are quite a pest in Australia, I believe, and are exterminated by the thousand; I have often wondered if a syndicate could not be formed to acquire the skins. This idea, so far as I know, is original, but you are quite welcome to it if——"

Mr. Selwyn rose abruptly to his feet.

"I once in my boyhood possessed a rabbit —of the lop-eared variety," I continued, "which over-ate itself and died. I remember I attempted to skin it with dire results——"

"Sir," said Mr. Selwyn, "I beg to inform you that I am not interested in rabbits, lop-eared or otherwise; nor do I propose to become so; furthermore——"

But at this moment of my triumph, even as he turned to depart, something small and white fluttered down from the branches above, and the next moment Selwyn had stooped and picked up a lace handkerchief. Then, while he stared at it and I at him, there came a ripple of laughter and Lisbeth peered down at us through the leaves.

"My handkerchief—thank you," she said, as Selwyn stood somewhat taken aback by her sudden appearance.

"The trees hereabouts certainly bear very remarkable, not to say delightful fruit," he said.

"And as you will remember, I was always

particularly fond of apple-trees," I inter-
polated.

"Mr. Selwyn," smiled Lisbeth, "let me
introduce you to Mr. Brent."

"Sir," I said, "I am delighted to make
your acquaintance; have heard Her Grace
of Chelsea speak of you—her friends are
mine, I trust?"

Mr. Selwyn's bow was rather more than
distant.

"I have already had the pleasure of
meeting this—this very original gentleman
before, and under rather peculiar circumstances, Miss Elizabeth," he said, and
forthwith plunged into an account of the
whole affair of the "ambushes," while
Lisbeth, perched upon her lofty throne
surveyed us with an ever-growing astonishment.

"Whatever does it all mean?" she enquired
as Mr. Selwyn made an end.

"You must know then," I explained,
leaning upon my quarter-staff, "the Imp
took it into his head to become Robin
Hood; I was Little-John, and Mr. Selwyn

here was so very obliging as to enact the rôle of Sheriff of Nottingham——"

"I beg your pardon," exclaimed Mr. Selwyn indignantly, turning upon me with a fiery eye.

"Everyone recollects the immortal exploits of Robin and his 'merrie men,'" I continued, "and you will, of course, remember that they had a habit of capturing the Sheriff and tying him up to trees and things. Naturally the Imp did not proceed to that extreme. He contented himself with merely capturing the Sheriff's hat. I think that you will agree that those 'ambushes' worked like a charm, Mr. Selwyn?"

"Miss Elizabeth," he said, disdaining any reply, "I am aware of the affection you lavish upon your nephew; I hope that you will take measures to restrain him from such pranks—such very disgraceful pranks —in the future. I myself should suggest a change of companionship" (here he glanced at me) "as the most salutary method. Good afternoon, Miss Elizabeth." So saying, Mr. Selwyn raised his hat, bowed stiffly to me, and, turning upon an indignant heel, strode haughtily away.

"Well!" exclaimed Lisbeth with a look of very real concern.

"Very well, indeed!" I nodded; "we are alone at last."

"Oh, Dick! but to have offended him like this!"

"A highly estimable young gentleman," I said, "though deplorably lacking in that saving sense of humour which——"

"Aunt Agatha seems to think a great deal of him."

"So I understand," I nodded.

"Only this morning I received a letter from her, in which, among other things, she pointed out what a very excellent match he would be."

"And what do you think?"

"Oh I agree with her, of course; his family dates back ages and ages before the Conqueror, and he has two or three estates besides Selwyn Park, and one in Scotland."

"Do you know, Lisbeth, that reminds me of another house—not at all big or splendid, but of great age; a house which stands not far from the village of Down, in Kent; a house which is going to rack and ruin for want of a mistress. Sometimes, just as evening comes on, I think it must dream of the light feet and gentle hands it has known so many years ago, and feels its loneliness more than ever."

"Poor old house!" said Lisbeth softly.

"Yes, a house is very human, Lisbeth, especially an old one, and feels the need of that loving care which only a woman can bestow, just as we do ourselves."

"Dear old house!" said Lisbeth, more softly than before.

"How much longer must it wait—when will you come and care for it, Lisbeth?"

She started, and I thought her cheeks seemed a trifle pinker than usual as her eyes met mine.

"Dick," she said wistfully, "I do wish you would get the ladder; it's horribly uncomfortable to sit in a tree for hours and——"

"First of all, Lisbeth, you will forgive the Imp—full and freely, won't you?"

"He shall go to bed without any tea whatever."

"That will be rank cruelty, Lisbeth; remember he is a growing boy."

"And I have been perched up here—between heaven and earth—all the afternoon."

"Then why not come down?" I inquired.

"If you will only get the ladder——"

"If you will just put your right foot in my——"

"I won't!" said Lisbeth.

"As you please," I nodded, and sitting down, mechanically took out my pipe and began to fill it, while she opened her book, frowning. And after she had read very studiously for perhaps two minutes, she drew out and consulted her watch. I did the same.

"A quarter to five!" I said.

Lisbeth glanced down at me with the air of one who is deliberating upon two courses of action, and when at length she spoke, every trace of irritation had vanished completely.

"Dick, I'm awfully hungry."

"So am I," I nodded.

"It *would* be nice to have tea here under the trees, wouldn't it?"

"It would be positively idyllic!" I said.

"Then if you will please find that ladder——"

"If you will promise to forgive the Imp——"

"Certainly not!" she retorted.

"So be it!" I sighed, and sat down again. As I did so she launched her book at me.

"Wretch!" she exclaimed.

"Which means that you are ready to descend?" I inquired, rising and depositing the maltreated volume side by side with my pipe on a rustic table near by; "very good. Place your right foot in——"

"Oh, all right," she said quite pettishly, and next moment I had her in my arms.

"Dick! put me down—at once!"

"One moment, Lisbeth; that boy is a growing boy——"

c

"And shall go to bed without any tea!" she broke in.

"Very well, then," I said, and reading the purpose in my eyes, she attempted, quite vainly, to turn her head aside.

"You will find it quite useless to struggle, Lisbeth," I warned. "Your only course is to remember that he is a growing boy."

"And you are a brute!" she cried.

"Undoubtedly," I answered, bending my head nearer her petulant lips. "But think of the Imp in bed, lying there, sleepless, tealess and growing all the while as fast as he can."

Lisbeth surrendered, of course, but my triumph was greatly tempered with disappointment.

"You will then forgive him for the 'ambushes' and cherish him with much tea?" I stipulated, winking away a tress of hair that tickled most provokingly.

"Yes," said Lisbeth.

"And no bed until the usual hour?"

"No," she answered, quite subdued; "and

now please do put me down." So I sighed and perforce obeyed.

She stood for a moment patting her rebellious hair into order with deft, white fingers, looking up at me meanwhile with a laugh in her eyes that seemed almost a challenge. I took a hasty step toward her, but as I did so the Imp hove into view.

"Hallo, Auntie Lisbeth!" he exclaimed, eyeing her wonderingly; then his glance wandered round as if in quest of something.

"How did she do it, Uncle Dick?" he inquired.

"Do what, my Imp?"

"Why, get out of the tree?"

I smiled and looked at Lisbeth.

"Did she climb down?"

"No," said I, shaking my head.

"Did she—jump down?"

"No, she didn't jump down."

"Well, did she—did she fly down?"

"No, nor fly down—she just came down."

"Yes, but how did she——"

"Reginald," said Lisbeth, "run and tell the maids to bring tea out here—for three."

"Three?" echoed the Imp. "But Dorothy has gone out to tea, you know—is Uncle Dick going to——"

"To be sure, Imp," I nodded.

"Oh, that is fine—hurrah, Little-John!" he cried, and darted off.

"And you, Lisbeth?" I said imprisoning her hands. "Are you glad also?"

Lisbeth did not speak, yet I was satisfied nevertheless.

CHAPTER III

THE DESPERADOES

FANE COURT stands bowered in trees, with a wide stretch of the greenest of green lawns sloping down to the river stairs.

They are quaint old stairs, with a marble rail and carved balusters, worn and crumbling, yet whose decay is half hid by the kindly green of lichens and mosses; stairs indeed for an idle fellow to dream over on a hot summer's afternoon—and they were, moreover, a favourite haunt of Lisbeth. It was here that I had moored my boat, therefore, and now lay back, pipe in mouth and with a cushion beneath my head, in that blissful state between sleeping and waking.

Now, as I lay, from the blue wreaths of my pipe I wove me fair fancies:

And lo! the stairs were no longer deserted; there were fine gentlemen, patched and powdered in silks and satins, with shoe buckles that flashed in the sun; there were dainty ladies in quilted petticoats and flowered gowns, with most wonderful coiffures; and there was Lisbeth, fairer and daintier than them all, and there, too, was I. And behold how demurely she curtsied and smiled behind her ivory fan! With what a grace I took a pinch of snuff! With what an air I bowed with hand on heart! Then, somehow, it seemed we were alone, she on the top stair, I on the lower. And standing thus I raised my arms to her with an appealing gesture. Her eyes looked down into mine, the patch quivered at the corner of her scarlet mouth, and there beside it was the dimple. Beneath her petticoat I saw her foot in a little pink satin shoe come slowly toward me and stop again. I watched, scarce breathing, for it seemed my fate hung in the balance. Would she come down to Love and me, or——

"Ship ahoy!" cried a voice, and in that moment my dream vanished. I sighed, and looking round, beheld a head peering at me over the balustrade—a head bound up in a bandanna handkerchief of large pattern and vivid colouring.

"Why, Imp!" I exclaimed. But my surprise abated when he emerged into full view.

About his waist was a broad-buckled belt, which supported a wooden cutlass, two or three murderous wooden daggers and a brace of toy pistols; while upon his legs were a pair of top-boots many sizes too large for him, so that walking required no little care. Yet on the whole his appearance was decidedly effective. There could be no mistake—he was a blood-thirsty pirate!

The Imp is an artist to his grimy finger-tips.

"Avast, shipmate!" I cried. "How's the wind?"

"Oh," he exclaimed, falling over his boots with eagerness, "do take me in your boat, an' let's be pirates, will you, Uncle Dick?"

"Well, that depends. Where is your Auntie Lisbeth?"

"Mr. Selwyn is going to row her and Dorothy up the river."

"Oh! he is!"

"Yes, an' they won't take me."

"Why not, my Imp?"

"'Cause they're 'fraid I should upset the boat. So I thought I'd come an' ask you to be a pirate, you know. I'll lend you my best dagger an' one of my pistols. Will you, Uncle Dick?"

"Come aboard, shipmate, if you are for Hispaniola, the Tortugas, and the Spanish Main," said I, whereupon he scrambled in, losing a boot overboard in his haste, which necessitated much intricate angling with the boathook ere it was recovered.

"They're Peter's, you know," he explained, as he emptied out the water. "I took them out of the harness-room; a pirate must have boots, you know, but I'm afraid Peter'll say things."

"Not a doubt of it when he sees them," I said as we pushed off.

"I wish," he began, looking round thought-fully after a minute or so, "I wish we could get a plank or a yard-arm from somewhere."

"What for, my Imp?"

"Why, don't you remember, pirates always had a plank for people to 'walk,' you know, an' used to 'swing them up to the yard-arm'?"

"You seem to know all about it," I said, as I pulled slowly down stream.

"Oh yes; I read it all in *Scarlet Sam, the Scourge of the South Seas*. Scarlet Sam was fine. He used to stride up and down the quarterdeck an' flourish his cutlass, an' his eyes would roll, an' he'd foam at the mouth, an'——"

"Knock everybody into the 'lee scuppers,'" I put in.

"Yes," cried the Imp in a tone of unfeigned surprise. "How did you know that, Uncle Dick?"

"Once upon a time," I said, as I swung lazily at the sculls, "I was a boy myself, and read a lot about a gentleman named 'Beetle-browed Ben.' I tell you, Imp, he was a terror for foaming and stamping, if you like, and used to flog three or four people every morning, just to get an appetite for breakfast." The Imp regarded me with round eyes.

"And then he was a very wonderful man in other ways. You see, he was always getting himself shot through the head, or run through the body, but it never hurt Beetle-browed Ben—not a bit of it."

"And did he 'swing people at the yard-arm—with a bitter smile'?"

"Lots of 'em!" I answered.

"An' make them 'walk the plank—with a horrid laugh'?"

"By the hundreds!"

"An' 'maroon them on a desolate island—with a low chuckle'?"

"Many a time," I answered; "and generally with a chuckle."

"Oh, I should like to read about him!" said the Imp with a deep sigh; "will you lend me your book about him, Uncle Dick?"

I shook my head. "Unfortunately, that, together with many other valued possessions, has been ravaged from me by the ruthless maw of Time," I replied sadly.

The Imp sat plunged in deep thought, trailing his fingers pensively in the water.

"And so your Auntie Lisbeth is going for a row with Mr. Selwyn, is she?" I said.

"Yes, an' I told her she could come an' be a pirate with me if she liked—but she wouldn't."

"Strange!" I murmured.

"Uncle Dick, do you think Auntie Lisbeth is in love with Mr. Selwyn?"

"What?" I exclaimed, and stopped rowing.

"I mean, do you think Mr. Selwyn is in love with Auntie Lisbeth?"

"My Imp, I'm afraid he is. Why?"

"'Cause cook says he is, an' so does Jane, an' they know all about love, you know. I've heard them read it out of a book lots an' lots of times. But I think love is awfull' silly, don't you, Uncle Dick?"

"Occasionally I greatly fear so," I sighed.

"You wouldn't go loving anybody, would you, Uncle Dick?"

"Not if I could help it," I answered, shaking my head; "but I do love someone, and that's the worst of it."

"Oh!" exclaimed the Imp, but in a tone more of sorrow than anger.

"Don't be too hard on me, Imp," I said; "your turn may come when you are older; you may love somebody one of these days."

The Imp frowned and shook his head. "No," he answered sternly; "when I grow up big I shall keep ferrets. Ben, the gardener's boy, has one with the littlest, teeniest pink nose you ever saw."

"Certainly a ferret has its advantage," I mused. "A ferret will not frown upon one one minute and flash a dimple at one the next. And then, again, a ferret cannot be reasonably supposed to possess an aunt. There is something to be said for your idea after all, Imp."

"Why, then, let's be pirates, Uncle Dick, he said with an air of finality. "I think I'll be Scarlet Sam, 'cause I know all about him, an' you can be Timothy Bone, the boatswain."

"Aye, aye, sir," I responded promptly; "only I say, Imp, don't roll your eyes

so frightfully or you may roll yourself overboard."

Scorning reply, he drew his cutlass, and
setting it between his teeth in most approved
pirate fashion, sat, pistol in hand, frowning
frantically at creation in general.

"Starboard your helm—starboard!" he
cried, removing his weapon for the purpose.

"Starboard it is!" I answered.

"Clear away for action!" growled the
Imp. "Double-shot the carronades, and,
bo'sun, pipe all hands to quarters."

Hereupon I executed a lively imitation
of a boatswain's whistle.

Most children are blessed with imagination, but the Imp in this respect is gifted
beyond his years. For him there is no such
thing as "pretence"; he has but to close
his eyes a moment to open them upon a new
and a very real world of his own—the golden
world of Romance, wherein so few of us are
privileged to walk in these cold days of
common sense. And yet it is a very fair
world, peopled with giants and fairies; where
castles lift their grim, embattled towers;

where magic woods and forests cast their shade, full of strange beasts; where knights ride forth with lance in rest and their armour shining in the sun. And right well we know them. There is Roland, Sir William Wallace, and Hereward the Wake; Ivanhoe, the Black Knight, and bold Robin Hood. And there, too, is King Arthur with his Knights of the Round Table—but the throng is very great, and who could name them all?

So the Imp and I sailed away into this wonderful world of romance aboard our gallant vessel, which, like any other pirate ship that ever existed—in books or out of them—"luffed, and filling upon another tack, stood away in pursuit of the Spanish treasure galleon in the offing."

What pen could justly describe the fight which followed—how guns roared and pistols flashed, while the air was full of shouts and cries and the thundering din of battle; how Scarlet Sam foamed and stamped and flourished his cutlass; how Timothy Bone piped his whistle as a bo'sun should? We had already sunk five great galleons and were hard at work with a sixth, which was evidently in a bad way, when Scarlet Sam ceased foaming and pointed over my shoulder with his dripping blade.

"Sail ho!" he cried.

"Where away?" I called back.

"Three points on the weather bow."

As he spoke came the sound of oars, and turning my head, I saw a skiff approaching, sculled by a man in irreproachable flannels and straw hat.

"Why, it's—it's him!" cried the Imp suddenly. "Heave to, there!" he bellowed in the voice of Scarlet Sam. "Heave to, or I'll sink you!" Almost with the words, and before I could prevent him, he gave a sharp tug to the rudder-lines; there was an angry exclamation behind me, a shock, a splintering of wood, and I found myself face to face with Mr. Selwyn, flushed and hatless.

Mr. Selwyn exclaimed, and proceeded to fish for his hat with the shaft of his broken oar.

The Imp sat for a moment half frightened at his handiwork, then rose to his feet, cutlass in hand, but I punted him gently back into his seat with my foot.

"Really," I began, "I'm awfully sorry, you know—er——"

"May I inquire," said Mr. Selwyn cuttingly, as he surveyed his dripping hat—"may I inquire how it all happened?"

"A most deplorable accident, I assure you. If I can tow you back I shall be delighted, and as for the damage——"

"The damage is trifling, thanks," he returned icily; "it is the delay that I find annoying."

"You have my very humblest apologies," I said meekly. "If I can be of any service——" Mr. Selwyn stopped me with a wave of his hand.

"Thank you, I think I can manage," he said; "but I should rather like to know how it happened. You are unused to rowing, I presume?"

"Sir," I answered, "it was chiefly owing to the hot-headedness of Scarlet Sam, the Scourge of the South Seas."

"I beg your pardon?" said Mr. Selwyn with raised brows.

"Sir," I went on, "at this moment you probably believe yourself to be Mr. Selwyn of Selwyn Park. Allow me to dispel that illusion; you are, on the contrary, Don Pedro Vasquez da Silva, commanding the *Esmeralda* galleasse, bound out of Santa Cruz. In us you behold Scarlet Sam and Timothy Bone, of the good ship *Black Death*, with the 'skull and cross-bones' fluttering at our peak. If you don't see it, that is not our fault."

Mr. Selwyn stared at me in wide-eyed astonishment, then shrugging his shoulders, turned his back upon me and paddled away as best he might.

"Well, Imp," I said, "you've done it this time!"

"'Fraid I have," he returned; "but oh! wasn't it grand—and all that about Don Pedro an' the treasure galleon! I do wish I knew as much as you do, Uncle Dick. I'd be a real pirate then."

"Heaven forfend!" I exclaimed.

So I presently turned and rowed back up-stream, not a little perturbed in my mind as to the outcome of the adventure.

"Not a word, mind!" I cautioned as I caught sight of a certain dainty figure watching our approach from the shade of her parasol. The Imp nodded, sighed, and sheathed his cutlass.

"Well!" said Lisbeth as we glided up to the water-stairs; "I wonder what mischief you have been after together?"

"We have been floating upon a river of dreams," I answered, rising and lifting my hat; "we have likewise discoursed of many things. In the words of the immortal Carroll:

"'Of shoes, and ships, and sealing-wax, and cabbages, and——'"

"Pirates!" burst out the Imp.

"This dream river of ours," I went on, quelling him with a glance, "has carried us to you, which is very right and proper. Dream rivers always should, more especially when you sit

"'Mid sunshine throned, and all alone.'"

"But I'm not all alone, Dick."

"No; I'm here," said a voice, and Dorothy appeared with her small and very fluffy kitten under her arm as usual. "We are waiting for Mr. Selwyn, you know. We've waited, oh! a long, long time, but he hasn't come, and Auntie says he's a wretch and——"

"Dorothy!" exclaimed Lisbeth frowning.

"Yes, you did, Auntie," said Dorothy, nodding her head. "I heard you when Louise ran up a tree and I had to coax her back; and I have a clean frock on, too, and Louise will be, oh, so disappointed!" Here she kissed the fluffy kitten on the nose. "So he is a wretch; don't you think so, Uncle Dick?"

"Such delay is highly reprehensible," I nodded.

"I'm glad you've come, Uncle Dick, and so is Auntie. She was hoping——"

"That will do, Dorothy!" Lisbeth interrupted.

"I wonder what she was hoping?" I sighed.

"If you say another word, Dorothy, I won't tell you any more about the Fairy Prince," said Lisbeth.

"Why, then," I continued, seeing the threat had the desired effect, "since Mr. Selwyn hasn't turned up, perhaps you would care to——"

—"Be a pirate!" put in the Imp.

"To come for a row with us?" I corrected.

—"Aboard the good ship *Black Death*," he went on, "'with the skull an' crossbones at our peak.'"

"Thanks," said Lisbeth, "but really, I don't think I should. What a horrible name!"

"What's in a name? a boat by any other——" I misquoted. "If you like, we'll call it the *Joyful Hope*, bound for the Land of Heart's Delight."

Lisbeth shook her head, but I fancied the dimple peeped at me for a moment.

"It would be a pity to disappoint Louise," I said, reaching up to stroke the fluffy kitten.

"Yes," cried Dorothy, "do let's go, Auntie."

"For the sake of Louise," I urged and held out my arms to her. Lisbeth was standing on the top stair and I on the lower, in exactly the same attitudes as I had beheld in my vision. I saw her foot come slowly toward me and stop again; her red lips quivered into a smile, and lo, there was the dimple! Dorothy saw it, too—children are wonderfully quick in such matters—and next moment was ensconced in the boat, Louise in her lap, and there was nothing left for Lisbeth but to follow.

The Imp went forward to keep a "lookout," and finding a length of fishing-line, announced his intention of "heaving the lead."

I have upon several occasions ridden with Lisbeth—she is a good horsewoman—frequently danced with her, but never before had I been with her in a boat. The novelty of it was therefore decidedly pleasing, the more so as she sat so close that by furtively reaching out a foot I could just touch the hem of her dress.

"Uncle Dick," said Dorothy, looking up

at me with her big grey eyes, "where is the Land of Heart's Delight?"

"It lies beyond the River of Dreams," I answered.

"Is it far away?"

"I'm afraid it is, Dorothy."

"Oh!—and hard to get to?"

"Yes; though it depends altogether upon who is at the helm."

Lisbeth very slowly began to tie a knot in the rudder-line.

"Well, Auntie's steering now. Could she get us there?"

"Yes, she could get us there, if she would."

"Oh!" cried Dorothy, "do—do steer for the Land of Heart's Delight, Auntie Lisbeth; it sounds so pretty, and I'm sure Louise would like it ever so much."

But Lisbeth only laughed, and tied another knot in the rudder-line.

"The Land of Heart's Delight!" repeated Dorothy. "It sounds rather like Auntie's tale of the Fairy Prince. His name was Trueheart."

"And what was Prince Trueheart like?"
I inquired.

"Fine!" broke in the Imp. "He used
to fight dragons, you know."

"And he lived in a palace of crystal,"
continued Dorothy, "and he was so good
and kind that the birds used to make friends
with him!"

"An' he wore gold armour, an' a big
feather in his helmet!" supplemented the
Imp.

"And of course he loved the beautiful
princess," I ended.

"Yes," nodded Dorothy; "but how did
you know there was a beautiful princess?"

"Uncle Dick knows everything, of course,"
returned the Imp sententiously.

"Do you think the beautiful princess loved
the prince, Dorothy?" I asked, glancing at
Lisbeth's averted face.

"Well," answered Dorothy, pursing her
mouth thoughtfully. "I don't know, Uncle
Dick; you see, Auntie hasn't got to that
yet, but everybody loves somebody some-
time, you know. Betty—she's our cook,

you know—Betty says all nice tales end up in marrying and living happy ever after."

"Not a doubt of it," said I, resting on my oars. "What do you think, Lisbeth?" She leaned back and regarded me demurely beneath her long lashes for a moment.

"I think," she answered, "that it would be much nicer if you would go on rowing."

"One more question," I said. "Tell me, has this Prince Trueheart got a moustache?"

"Like Mr. Selwyn?" cried the Imp; "should think not. The prince was a fine chap, an' used to kill dragons, you know."

"Ah! I'm glad of that," I murmured, passing my fingers across my shaven upper lip; "very glad indeed."

Lisbeth laughed, but I saw her colour deepen, and she looked away.

"Oh, it must be lovely to kill a dragon!" sighed the Imp.

Now, as he spoke, chancing to look round, I saw in the distance a man in a boat, who rowed most lustily—and the man wore a Panama.

Hereupon, taking a fresh grip upon my long sculls, I began to row—to row, indeed, as I had not done for many a year, with a long, steady stroke that made the skiff fairly leap.

Who does not know that feeling of exhilaration as the blades grip the water and the gentle lapping at the bow swells into a gurgling song? The memorable time when I had "stroked" Cambridge to victory was nothing to this. Then it was but empty glory that hung in the balance, while now——!

I settled my feet more firmly, and lengthening my stroke, pulled with a will. Lisbeth sat up, and I saw her fingers tighten upon the rudder-line.

"You asked me to row, you know," I said in response to her look.

"Yo-ho!" roared Scarlet Sam in the gruffest of nautical tones. "By the deep nine, an' the wind's a-lee, so heave, my mariners all—O!"

At first we began to gain considerably upon our pursuer, but presently I saw him turn his head, saw the Panama tossed aside

as Mr. Selwyn settled down to real business—
and the struggle began.

Very soon, probably owing to the fixedness
of my gaze, or my unremitting exertion or
both, Lisbeth seemed to become aware of
the situation, and turned to look over her
shoulder. I set my teeth as I waited to
meet her indignant look, for I had determined to continue the struggle, come what
might. But when at last she did confront
me her eyes were shining, her cheeks were
flushed, and there was actually—the dimple.

"Sit still, children," she said, and that
was all; but for one moment her eyes looked
into mine.

The old river has witnessed many a hard-
fought race in its time, but never was there
one more hotly contested than this. Never
was the song of the water more pleasant to
my ear, never was the spring and bend of
the long sculls more grateful, as the banks
swept by faster and faster. No pirate
straining every inch of canvas to escape
well-merited capture, no smuggler fleeing
for some sheltered cove, with the revenue

cutter close astern, ever experienced a keener excitement than did we.

The Imp was in a perfect ecstasy of delight; even Dorothy forgot her beloved Louise for the time, while Lisbeth leaned toward me, the tiller-lines over her shoulders, her lips parted and a light in her eyes I had never seen there before. And yet Selwyn hung fast in our rear. If he was deficient in a sense of humour, he could certainly row.

"He was an Oxford Blue," said Lisbeth, speaking almost in a whisper, "and he has an empty boat!"

I longed to kiss the point of her little tan shoe or the hem of her dress for those impulsive words, and tried to tell her so with my eyes—breath was too precious just then. Whether she understood or not I won't be sure, but I fancy she did from the way her lashes drooped.

"Oh, my eyes!" bellowed Scarlet Sam; "keep her to it, quartermaster, an' take a turn at the mizzen-shrouds!"

When I again glanced at our pursuer I saw that he was gaining. Yes, there could be no mistake; slowly but surely, try as I would, the distance between us lessened and lessened, until he was so near that I could discern the very parting of his black hair. So perforce, bowing to the inevitable, I ceased my exertions, contenting myself with a long, easy stroke. Thus by the time he was alongside I had in some measure regained my breath.

"Miss—Eliz—beth," he panted, very hot of face and moist of brow, "must beg—the—favour—of few words with you."

"With pleasure, Mr. Selwyn," answered Lisbeth, radiant with smiles; "as many as you wish." Forthwith Mr. Selwyn panted out his indictment against the desperadoes of the *Black Death*, while the Imp glanced apprehensively from him to Lisbeth and stole his hand furtively into mine.

"I should not have troubled you with this, Miss Elizabeth," Selwyn ended, "but that I would not have you think me neglectful of an appointment, especially with you."

"Indeed, Mr. Selwyn, I am very grateful to you for opening my eyes to such a—a——"

"Very deplorable accident," I put in.

"I—I was perfectly certain," she continued, without so much as glancing in my direction, "that you would never have kept me waiting without sufficient reason. And now, Mr. Brent, if you will be so obliging as to take us to the bank, Mr. Selwyn shall row us back—if he will."

"Delighted!" he murmured.

"I ordered tea served in the orchard at five o'clock," smiled Lisbeth, "and it is only just four, so——"

"Which bank would you prefer," I inquired—"the right or the left?"

"The nearest," said Lisbeth.

"Which should you think was the nearest, Mr. Selwyn?" I queried.

Disdaining any reply, Selwyn ran his skiff ashore, and I obediently followed. Without waiting for my assistance, Lisbeth deftly made the exchange from one boat to the other, followed more slowly by Dorothy.

"Come, Reginald," she said, as Selwyn made ready to push off; "we're waiting for you." The Imp squatted closer to me.

"Reginald Augustus!" said Lisbeth. The Imp shuffled uneasily.

"Are you coming?" inquired Lisbeth.

"I—I'd rather be a pirate with Uncle Dick please, Auntie Lisbeth," he said at last.

"Very well," nodded Lisbeth with an air of finality; "then of course I must punish you." But her tone was strangely gentle, and as she turned away I'll vow I saw the ghost of that dimple—yes, I'll vow it.

So we sat very lonely and dejected, the Imp and I, desperadoes though we were, as we watched Selwyn's boat grow smaller and smaller until it was lost round a bend in the river.

"'Spect I shall get sent to bed for this," said the Imp after a long pause.

"I think it more than probable, my Imp."

"But then, it was a very fine race— oh, beautiful!" he sighed; "an' I couldn't desert my ship an' Timothy Bone, an' leave you here all by yourself—now could I, Uncle Dick?"

"Of course not, Imp."

"What are you thinking about, Uncle Dick?" he inquired, as I stared, chin in hand, at nothing in particular.

"I was wondering, Imp, where the River of Dreams was going to lead me, after all."

"To the Land of Heart's Delight, of course," he answered promptly; "you said so, you know, an' you never tell lies. Uncle Dick—never."

CHAPTER IV

AT THE THREE JOLLY ANGLERS

THE Three Jolly Anglers is an inn of a distinctly jovial aspect, with its toppling gables, its creaking sign, and its bright lattices, which, like merry little twinkling eyes, look down upon the eternal river to-day with the same half-waggish, half-kindly air as they have done for generations.

Upon its battered sign, if you look closely enough, you may still see the Three Anglers themselves, somewhat worn and dim with time and stress of weather, yet preserving their jollity through it all with an heroic fortitude—as they doubtless will do until they fade away altogether.

It is an inn with raftered ceilings and narrow, winding passageways; an inn with long low chambers full of unexpected nooks and corners, with great four-post beds built for tired giants it would seem, and wide deep chimneys reminiscent of Gargantuan rounds of beef; an inn whose very walls seem to exude comfort, as it were—the solid comfortable comfort of a bygone age.

Of all the many rooms here to be found I love best that which is called the Sanded Parlour. Never were wainscoted walls of a mellower tone, never was pewter more gleaming, never were things more bright and speckless, from the worn quaint andirons on the hearth to the brass-bound blunderbuss, with the two ancient fishing rods above. At one end of the room was a long, low casement, and here I leaned, watching the river near by, and listening to its never-ceasing murmur. I had dined an hour ago; the beef had been excellent—it always is at the Three Jolly Anglers; also my pipe seemed to have an added flavour.

Yet, despite all this, I did not enjoy that supreme content—that philosophical calm which such beef and such surroundings surely warranted. But then, who ever

D

heard of Love and Philosophy going together?

Away over the uplands a round harvest moon was beginning to rise, flecking the shadowy waters with patches of silver, and, borne to my ears upon the warm still air, came the throb of distant violins. This served only to deepen my melancholy, reminding me that somebody or other was giving a ball to-night; and Lisbeth was there, and Mr. Selwyn was there, of course, and I—I was here—alone with the brass-bound blunderbuss, the ancient fishing-rods, and the antique andirons on the hearth; with none to talk to save the moon, and the jasmine that had crept in at the open casement. And, noting the splendour of the night, I experienced towards Lisbeth a feeling of pained surprise that she should prefer the heat and garish glitter of a ballroom to walking beneath such a moon with me.

Indeed, it was a wondrous night! one of these warm still nights which seem full of vague and untold possibilities! A night with magic in the air, when elves and fairies dance within their grassy rings, or, hiding amid the shade of trees, peep out at one between the leaves; or again, some gallant knight on mighty steed may come pacing slowly from the forest shadows, with the moonlight bright upon his armour.

Yes, surely there was magic in the air to-night! I half-wished that some enchanter might, by a stroke of his fairy wand, roll back the years and leave me in the brutal, virile, Good Old Times, when men wooed and won their loves by might and strength of arm, and not by gold, as is so often the case in these days of ours. To be mounted upon my fiery steed, lance in hand and sword on thigh, riding down the leafy alleys of the woods yonder, led by the throbbing, sighing melody. To burst upon the astonished dancers like a thunder-clap; to swing her up to my saddle-bow, and, clasped in each other's arms, to plunge into the green mystery of forest.

My fancies had carried me thus far when I became aware of a small furtive figure dodging from one patch of shadow to another. Leaning from the window I made out the form of a somewhat disreputable urchin, who, dropping upon hands and knees, proceeded to crawl towards me over the grass with a show of the most elaborate caution.

"Hallo!" I exclaimed, "halt and give the counter-sign!" The urchin sat up on his heels and stared at me with a pair of very round bright eyes.

"Please, are you Mr. Uncle Dick?" he inquired.

"Oh," I said, "you come from the Imp, I presume." The boy nodded a round head, at the same time fumbling with something in his pocket.

"And who may you be?" I inquired conversationally.

"I'm Ben, I am."

"The gardener's boy?" Again the round head nodded acquiescence as with much writhing and twisting he succeeded in drawing a heterogeneous collection of articles from his pocket, whence he selected a very dirty and clumpled piece of paper.

"He wants a ladder so's he can git out, but it's too big fer me to lift, so he told me to give you this here so's you would come an' rescue him—please, Mr. Uncle Dick." With which lucid explanation Ben handed me the crumpled note.

Spreading it out upon the window-sill, I managed to make out as follows:

"DEAR UNKEL DICK,—I'm riting this with my hart's blood bekors I'm a prisner in a gloomie dungun. It isn't really my heart's blood it's only red ink, so don't worry. Aunty lisbath cent me to bed just after tea bekors she said i'm norty, and when she'd gone Nurse locked me in so i can't get out and i'm tired of being a prisner, so please i want you to get the ladda and let me eskape, please unkel dick, will you.—yours till deth.

REGINALD AUGUSTUS."

"Auntie was reading *Ivanhoe* to us and i've been the Black Knight and you can be Gurth, the swine-herd, if you like."

"So that's the way of it?" I said. "Well! well! such an appeal shall not go unanswered, at least. Wait there, my trusty Benjamin, and I'll be with you anon." Pausing only to refill my tobacco-pouch and get my cap, I sallied out into the fragrant night, and set off along the river, the faithful Benjamin trotting at my heels.

Very soon we were skirting blooming flower-beds and crossing trim lawns, until at length we reached a certain wing of the house, from a window of which a pillow-case was dangling by means of a string.

"That's for provisions!" volunteered Ben. "We pretended he was starving, so he lets it down, an' I fill it with onions out of the vegetable garden."

At this moment the curly head of the Imp appeared at the window, followed by the major portion of his person.

"Oh, Uncle Dick!" he cried, in a loud stage-whisper, "I think you had better be the Black Knight, 'cause you're so big, you know."

"Imp," I said, "get in at once! Do you want to break your neck?"

The Imp obediently wriggled into safety.

"The ladder's in the tool-house, Uncle Dick—Ben'll show you. Will you get it, please?" he pleaded in a wheedling tone.

"First of all, my Imp, why did your Auntie Lisbeth send you to bed—had you been a very naughty boy?"

"No-o," he answered, after a moment's pause, "I don't think I was so very naughty— I only painted Dorothy like an Indian chief—green, with red spots, an' she looked fine, you know."

"Green, with red spots!" I repeated.

"Yes; only Auntie didn't seem to like it."

"I fear your Auntie Lisbeth lacks an eye for colour."

"Yes, 'fraid so; she sent me to bed for it, you know."

"Still, Imp, under the circumstances, I think it would be best if you got undressed and went to sleep."

"Oh, but I can't, Uncle Dick!"

"Why not, my Imp?"

"'Cause the moon's so very bright, an' everything looks so fine down there, an' I'm sure there's fairies about—Moon-fairies, you know—and I'm miserable."

"Miserable, Imp?"

"Yes, Auntie Lisbeth never came to kiss me good-night, an' so I can't go to sleep, Uncle Dick!"

"Why, that alters the case, certainly."

"Yes, an' the ladder's in the tool-house."

"Imp," I said, as I turned to follow Benjamin, "oh, you Imp!"

There are few things in this world more difficult to manage than a common or garden ladder; among other peculiarities it has a most unpleasant knack of kicking out suddenly just as everything appears to be going smoothly, which is apt to prove disconcerting to the novice. However, after sundry mishaps of the kind, I eventually got it reared up to the window, and a moment afterwards the Imp had climbed down and stood beside me, drawing the breath of freedom.

As a precautionary measure we proceeded to hide the ladder in a clump of rhododendrons hard by, and had but just done so when Benjamin uttered a cry of warning and took to his heels, while the Imp and I sought shelter behind a friendly tree. And not a whit too soon, for, scarcely had we done so, when two figures came round a corner of the house—two figures who walked very slowly and very close together.

"Why, it's Betty—the cook, you know—an' Peter!" whispered the Imp.

Almost opposite our hiding-place Betty paused to sigh heavily and stare up at the moon.

"Oh, Peter!" she murmured, "look at that there orb!"

"Ar!" said Peter, gazing obediently upward.

"Peter, ain't it 'eavingly; don't it stir your very soul?"

"Ar!" said Peter.

"Peter, are you sure you loves me more than that Susan thing at the doctor's?"

A corduroy coat-sleeve crept slowly about Betty's plump waist, and there came the unmistakable sound of a kiss.

"Really and truly, Peter?"

"Ar!" said Peter.

The kissing sound was repeated, and they walked on once more, only closer than ever now on account of the corduroy coat-sleeve.

"Those two are in love, you know," nodded the Imp. "Peter says the cheese-cakes she makes are enough to drive any man into marrying her, whether he wants to or not, an' I heard Betty telling Jane that she adored Peter, 'cause he had so much soul! Why is it," he inquired thoughtfully as he watched the two out of sight, "why is it, Uncle Dick, that people in love alwavs look so silly?"

"Do you think so?" I asked, as I paused to light my pipe.

"'Course I do!" returned the Imp; "what's anyone got to put their arm round girls for, just as if they wanted holding up?—I think it's awfully silly!"

"Of course it is, Imp—your wisdom is unassailable. Still, do you know, I can understand a man being foolish enough to do it—occasionally."

"But you never would, Uncle Dick?"

"Alas, Imp!" I said, shaking my head, "Fortune seems to preclude all chances of it."

"'Course you wouldn't," he exclaimed; "an' Ivanhoe wouldn't——"

"Ah, but he did!" I put in; "have you forgotten Rowena?"

"Oh!" cried the Imp dolefully, "do you really think he ever put his arm round her?"

"Sure of it," I nodded.

The Imp seemed much cast down and even shocked.

"But there was the Black Knight," he said, brightening suddenly; "Richard of the Lion Heart, you know—he never did!"

"Not while he was fighting, of course, but afterwards, if history is to be believed, he very frequently did; and we are all alike, Imp—everybody does sooner or later."

"But why? Why should anyone want to put their arm round a girl, Uncle Dick?"

"For the simple reason that the girl is there to put it round, I suppose. And now, Imp, let us talk of fish."

Instinctively we had wandered towards the river, and now we stood to watch the broad, silver path made by the moon across the mystery of its waters.

"I love to see the shine upon the river like that," said the Imp dreamily; "Auntie Lisbeth says it's the path that the Moon-fairies come down by to bring you nice dreams when you've been good. I've got out of bed lots of times an' watched an' watched, but I've never seen them come. Do you think there are fairies in the moon, Uncle Dick?"

"Undoubtedly," I answered; "how else does it keep—so bright? I used to wonder once how they managed to make it shine so."

"It must need lots of rubbing!" said the Imp; "I wonder if they ever get tired?"

"Of course they do, Imp, and disheartened, too, sometimes, like the rest of us, and then everything is black, and people wonder where the moon is. But they are very brave, these Moon-fairies, and they never quite lose hope, you know so they presently go back to their rubbing and polishing, always starting at one edge. And in a little while we see it begin to shine again, very small and thin at first, like, a——"

"Thumb-nail!"

"Yes, just like a thumb-nail; and so they go on working and working at it until it gets as big and round and bright as it is to-night."

Thus we walked together through a fairy world, the Imp and I, while above the murmur of the waters, above the sighing of the trees, came the soft tremulous melody of the violins.

"I do wish I had lived when there were knights like Ivanhoe," burst out the Imp suddenly; "it must have been fine to knock a man off his horse with your lance."

"Always supposing he didn't knock you off first, Imp."

"Oh! I should have been the sort of knight that nobody could knock off, you know. An' I'd have wandered about on my faithful charger, fighting all sort of caddish barons and caitiffs, an' slaying giants;

an' I'd have rescued lovely ladies from castles grim—though I wouldn't have put my arm round them, of course!"

"Perish the thought, my Imp!"

"Uncle Dick!" he said insinuatingly, "I do wish you'd be the Black Knight, an' let me be Ivanhoe."

"But there are no caitiffs and things left for us to fight, Imp, and no lovely ladies to rescue from castles grim, alas!"

Now we had been walking on, drawn almost imperceptibly by the magic thread of the melody, which had led us, by devious paths, to a low stone wall, beyond which we could see the gleam of lighted windows and the twinkle of fairy lamps among the trees. And over there, amid the music and laughter, was Lisbeth in all the glory of her beauty, happy, of course, and light-hearted; and here, beneath the moon, was I.

"We could pretend this was a castle grim, you know, Uncle Dick, full of dungeons an' turrets, an' that we were going to rescue Auntie Lisbeth."

"Imp," I said, "that's really a great idea."

"I wish I'd brought my trusty sword," he sighed, searching about for something to supply its place; "I left it under my pillow, you know." Very soon, however, he had procured two sticks, somewhat thin and wobbly, yet which, by the magic of imagination, became transformed into formidable two-edged swords, with one of which he armed me, the other he flourished above his head.

"Forward, gallant knights!" he cried; "the breach! the breach! On! on! St. George for Merrie England!" With the words he clambered upon the wall and disappeared upon the other side.

For a moment I hesitated, and then, inspired by the music and the thought of Lisbeth, I followed suit. It was all very mad, of course, but who cared for sanity on such a night—certainly not I.

"Careful now, Imp!" I cautioned; "if anyone should see us they'll take us for thieves, or lunatics, beyond a doubt."

We found ourselves in an enclosed garden with a walk which led between rows of fruit trees. Following this, it brought us out upon a broad stretch of lawn, with here and there a great tree, and beyond, the gleaming windows of the house. Filled with the spirit of adventure, we approached, keeping in the shadow as much as possible, until we could see figures that strolled to and fro upon the terrace or promenaded the walks below.

The excitement of dodging our way among so many people was intense; time and again we were only saved from detection by more than one wandering couple, owing to the fact that all their attention was centred in themselves. For instance, we were skirmishing round a clump of laurels, to gain the shadow of the terrace, when we almost ran into the arms of a pair; but they didn't see us, for the very good reason that she was staring at the moon and he at her.

"So sweet of you, Archibald!" she was saying.

"What did she call him 'bald for, Uncle

Dick?" inquired the Imp in a loud stage-whisper, as I dragged him down behind the laurels. "He's not a bit bald, you know! An' I say, Uncle Dick, did you see his arm? It was round——"

"Yes—yes!" I nodded.

"Just like Peter's, you know."

"Yes—yes, I saw."

"I wonder why she called him——"

"Hush!" I broke in, "his name is Archibald, I suppose."

"Well, I hope when I grow up nobody will ever call me——"

"Hush!" I said again, "not a word—there's your Auntie Lisbeth!" She was, indeed, standing upon the terrace, within a yard of our hiding-place, and beside her was Mr. Selwyn.

"Uncle Dick," whispered the irrepressible Imp, "do you think if we watch long enough that Mr. Selwyn will put his arm round——"

"Shut up!" I whispered savagely.

Lisbeth was clad in a long, trailing gown of dove-coloured silk—one of those close-fitting garments that make the un-initiated, such as myself, wonder how they are ever got on.

Mr. Selwyn stood beside her with a plate of ice-cream in his hand, which he handed to her, and they sat down. As I watched her and noticed her weary, bored air, and how wistfully she gazed up at the silver disc of the moon, I experienced a feeling of decided satisfaction.

"Yes," said Lisbeth, toying absently with the ice-cream, "he painted Dorothy's face with stripes of red and green enamel, and goodness only knows how we can ever get it all off!"

Mr. Selwyn was duly shocked, and murmured something about the "efficacy of turpentine" in such an emergency.

"Of course, I had to punish him," continued Lisbeth, "so I sent him to bed immediately after tea, and never went to say good-night, or tuck him up as I usually do, and it has been worrying me all the evening."

Mr. Selwyn was sure that he was all right, and positively certain that at this moment

he was wrapped in balmy slumber. Despite
my warning grasp, the Imp chuckled, but
we were saved by the band striking up. Mr.
Selwyn rose, giving his arm to Lisbeth, and
they re-entered the ballroom. One by one
the other couples followed suit until the
long terrace was deserted.

Now, upon Lisbeth's deserted chair, show-
ing wonderfully pink in the soft glow of the
Chinese lanterns, was the ice-cream.

"Uncle Dick," said the Imp in his
thoughtful way, "I think I'll be a bandit for
a bit."

"Anything you like," I answered rashly,
"so long as we get away while we can."

"All right," he whispered, "I won't be a
minute," and before I could stop him he had
scrambled down the steps and fallen to upon
the ice-cream.

The wonderful celerity with which the
Imp wolfed down that ice-cream was positively awe-inspiring. In less time almost
than it takes to tell, the plate was empty.
Yet scarcely had he swallowed the last
mouthful when he heard Mr. Selwyn's

voice close by. In his haste the Imp dropped his cap, a glaring affair of red and white, and before he could recover it, Lisbeth reappeared, followed by Mr. Selwyn.

"It certainly is more pleasant out here!" he was saying.

Lisbeth came straight towards the cap—it was a moral impossibility that she could fail to see it—yet she sank into her chair without word or sign. Mr. Selwyn, on the contrary, stood with the empty ice plate in his hand, staring at it in wide-eyed astonishment.

"It's gone!" he exclaimed.

"Oh!" said Lisbeth.

"Most extraordinary!" said Mr. Selwyn, fixing his monocle and staring harder than ever; "I wonder where it can have got to?"

"Perhaps it melted!" Lisbeth suggested, "and I should so have loved an ice!" she sighed.

"Then, of course, I'll get you another, with pleasure," he said, and hurried off, eyeing the plate dubiously as he went.

No sooner was Lisbeth alone than she kicked aside the train of her dress and picked up the tell-tale cap.

"Imp!" she whispered, rising to her feet, "Imp, come here at once, sir!"

There was a moment's breathless pause, and then the Imp squirmed himself into view.

"Hallo, Auntie Lisbeth!" he said, with a cheerfulness wholly assumed.

"Oh!" she cried distressfully, "whatever does this mean; what are you doing here? Oh, you naughty boy!"

"Lisbeth," I said, as I rose in my turn and confronted her, "do not blame the child—the fault is mine—let me explain; by means of a ladder——"

"Not here," she whispered, glancing nervously towards the ballroom.

"Then come where I can."

"Impossible!"

"Not at all; you have only to descend these steps and we can talk undisturbed."

"Ridiculous!" she said, stooping to replace the Imp's cap; but being thus temptingly within reach, she was next moment beside us in the shadows.

"Dick, how could you, how dared you?"

"You see, I had to explain," I answered very humbly; "I really couldn't allow this poor child to bear the blame of my fault——"

"I'm not a 'poor child,' Uncle Dick," expostulated the Imp; "I'm a gallant knight and——"

"—The blame of my fault, Lisbeth," I continued. "I alone must face your just resentment, for——"

"Hush!" she whispered, glancing hastily about.

"—For, by means of a ladder, Lisbeth, a common or garden ladder——"

"Oh, do be quiet!" she said, and laid her hand upon my lips, which I immediately imprisoned there, but for a moment only; the next it was snatched away as there came the unmistakable sound of someone approaching.

"Come along, Auntie Lisbeth," whispered the Imp; "fear not, we'll rescue you."

Oh! surely there was magic in the air

to-night; for, with a swift, dexterous movement, Lisbeth had swept her long train
across her arm, and we were running hand
in hand, all three of us, running across lawns
and down winding paths between yew hedges,
sometimes so close together that I could
feel a tress of her fragrant hair brushing
my face with a touch almost like a caress.
Surely, surely, there was magic in the air
to-night!

Suddenly Lisbeth stopped, flushed and
panting.

"Well!" she exclaimed, staring from me
to the Imp, and back again, "was ever
anything so mad!"

"Everything is mad to-night," I said;
"it's the moon!"

"To think of my running away like this
with two—two——"

"Interlopers," I suggested.

"I really ought to be very, very angry
with you—both of you," she said, trying
to frown.

"No, don't be angry with us, Auntie
Lisbeth," pleaded the Imp, "'cause you are

a lovely lady in a castle grim, an' we are
two gallant knights, so we had to come an'
rescue you; an' you never came to kiss me
good-night, an' I'm awful' sorry 'bout painting
Dorothy's face—really!"

"Imp," cried Lisbeth, falling on her
knees, regardless of her silks and laces,
"Imp, come and kiss me." The Imp
drew out a decidedly grubby handkerchief, and, having rubbed his lips with
it, obeyed.

"Now, Uncle Dick!" he said, and offered
me the grubby handkerchief. Lisbeth
actually blushed.

"Reginald!" she exclaimed, "whatever put
such an idea into your head?"

"Oh! everybody's always kissing somebody, you know," he nodded; "an' it's
Uncle Dick's turn now."

Lisbeth rose from her knees and began
to pat her rebellious hair into order. Now,
as she raised her arms, her shawl very naturally slipped to the ground; and standing
there, with her eyes laughing up at me
beneath their dark lashes, with the moonlight

in her hair, she had never seemed quite so bewilderingly beautiful before.

"Dick," she said, "I must go back at once —before they miss me."

"Go back!" I repeated; "never—that is, not yet."

"But suppose anyone saw us!" she said, with a hairpin in her mouth.

"They shan't," I answered; "you will see to that, won't you, Imp?"

"'Course I will, Uncle Dick!"

"Then go you, Sir Knight, and keep faithful ward behind yon apple-tree, and let no base varlet hither come; that is, if you see anyone, be sure to tell me."

The Imp saluted and promptly disappeared behind the apple-tree in question, while I stood watching Lisbeth's dexterous fingers and striving to remember a line from Keats, descriptive of a beautiful woman in the moonlight. Before I could call it to mind, however, Lisbeth interrupted me.

"Don't you think you might pick up my shawl instead of staring at me as if I was——"

"The most beautiful woman in the world!" I put in.

"Who is catching her death of cold," she laughed, yet for all her light tone her eyes drooped before mine as I obediently wrapped the shawl about her, in the doing of which, my arm, being round her, very naturally stayed there, and—wonder of wonders, was not repulsed. And at this very moment, from the shadowy trees behind us, came the rich clear song of a nightingale.

Oh, most certainly the air was full of magic to-night!

"Dick," said Lisbeth very softly, as the trilling notes died away, "I thought one could only dream such a night as this is."

"And yet life might hold many such for you and me, if you would only let it, Lisbeth," I reminded her. She did not answer.

"Not far from the village of Down, in Kent," I began.

"There stands a house," she put in, staring up at the moon with dreamy eyes.

"Yes."

"A very old house, with twisted Tudor chimneys and pointed gables—you see, I have it all by heart, Dick—a house with wide stairways and long panelled chambers——"

"Very empty and desolate at present," I added. "And, amongst other things, there is a rose garden—they call it My Lady's Garden, Lisbeth, though no lady has trod its winding paths for years and years. But I have dreamed, many and many a time, that we stood among the roses, she and I, upon just such another night as this is. So I keep the old house ready and the gardens freshly trimmed, ready for my lady's coming; must I wait much longer, Lisbeth?" As I ended the nightingale took up the story, pleading my cause for me, filling the air with a melody now appealing, now commanding, until it gradually died away in one long note of passionate entreaty.

Lisbeth sighed and turned towards me, but as she did so, I felt a tug at my coat, and, looking round, beheld the Imp.

"Uncle Dick," he said, his eyes studiously averted, doubtless on account of the position of my arm, "here's Mr. Selwyn!"

With a sudden exclamation Lisbeth started from me and gathered up her skirts to run.

"Whereaway, my Imp?"

"Coming across the lawn."

"Reginald," I said solemnly, "listen to me; you must sally out upon him with lance in rest, tell him you are a Knight-errant, wishful to uphold the glory of that faire ladye, your Auntie Lisbeth, and, what-ever happens, you must manage to keep him away from here. Do you understand?"

"Yes; only I do wish I'd brought my trusty sword, you know," he sighed.

"Never mind that now, Imp."

"Will Auntie Lisbeth be quite——"

"She will be all right."

"I suppose if you put your arm——"

"Never mind my arm, Imp, go!"

"Then fare thee well!" said he, and, with a melodramatic flourish of his lance, trotted off.

"What did he mean about your arm, Dick?"

"Probably this," I answered, slipping it around her again.

"But you must get away at once," whispered Lisbeth; "if Mr. Selwyn should see you——"

"I intend that he shall. Oh, it will be quite simple; while he is talking to me you can get back to the——"

"Hush!" she whispered, laying her fingers on my lips; "listen!"

"Hallo, Mr. Selwyn!" came in the Imp's familiar tones.

"Why, good gracious!" exclaimed another voice, much too near to be pleasant, "what on earth are you doing here—and at this time of night?"

"Looking for base varlets!"

"Don't you know that all little boys—all nice little boys—should have been in bed hours ago?"

"But I'm not a nice little boy; I'm a Knight-errant; would you like to get a lance, Mr. Selwyn, an' break it with me to the glory of my Auntie Lisbeth?"

"The question is, what has become of her?" said Mr. Selwyn. We waited almost breathlessly for the answer.

"Oh! I 'specks she's somewhere looking at the moon; everybody looks at the moon, you know; Betty does, an' the lady with the man with a funny name 'bout being bald, an'——"

"I think you had better come up to the house," said Mr. Selwyn.

"Do you think you could get me an ice-cream if I did?" asked the Imp persuasively; "nice an' pink, you know, with——"

"An ice!" repeated Mr. Selwyn; "I wonder how many you have had already to-night?"

The time for action was come.

"Lisbeth," I said, "we must go; such happiness as this could not last; how should it? I think it is given us to dream over in less happy days. For me it will be a memory to treasure always, and yet there might be one thing more—a little thing, Lisbeth—can you guess?" She did not speak, but I saw the dimple come and go at the corner of her mouth, so I stooped and kissed her. For a moment, all too brief, we stood thus, with the glory of the moonlight about us; then I was hurrying across the lawn after Selwyn and the Imp.

"Ah, Mr. Selwyn!" I said as I overtook them, "so you have found him, have you?" Mr. Selwyn turned to regard me, surprise writ large upon him, from the points of his immaculate patent-leather shoes to the parting of his no less immaculate hair.

"So very good of you," I continued; "you see he is such a difficult object to recover when once he gets mislaid; really, I'm awfully obliged." Mr. Selwyn's attitude was politely formal. He bowed.

"What is it to-night?" he inquired. "Pirates?"

"Hardly so bad as that," I returned; "to-night the air is full of the clash of armour and the ring of steel; if you do not hear it, that is not our fault."

"An' the woods are full of caddish barons and caitiff knaves, you know, aren't they, Uncle Dick?"

"Certainly," I nodded, "with lance and spear-point twinkling through the gloom; but in the silver glory of the moon, Mr. Selwyn, walk errant damozels and ladyes faïre, and again, if you don't see them, the loss is yours." As I spoke, away upon the terrace a grey shadow paused a moment ere it was swallowed in the brilliance of the ballroom; seeing which I did not mind the slightly superior smile that curved Mr. Selwyn's very precise moustache; after all, my rhapsody had not been altogether thrown away.

As I ended, the opening bars of a waltz floated out to us. Mr. Selwyn glanced back over his shoulder.

"Eh! I suppose you can find your way out?" he inquired.

"Oh yes, thanks."

"Then if you will excuse me, I think I'll leave you to—ah—to do it; the next dance is beginning, and—ah——"

"Certainly," I said, "of course—good-night, and much obliged—really!"

Mr. Selwyn bowed, and, turning away, left us to our own resources.

"I should have liked another ice, Uncle Dick," sighed the Imp regretfully.

"Knights never ate ice-cream!" I said, as we set off along the nearest path.

"Uncle Dick," said the Imp suddenly, "do you s'pose Mr. Selwyn wants to put his arm round Auntie Lis——"

"Possibly!"

"An' do you s'pose that Auntie Lisbeth wants Mr. Selwyn to——"

"I don't know—of course not—er—kindly shut up, will you, Imp?"

"I only wanted to know, you know," he murmured.

Therewith we walked on in silence, and I fell to dreaming of Lisbeth again, of how she had sighed, of the look in her eyes as she turned to me with her answer trembling on her lips—the answer which the Imp had inadvertently cut short.

In this frame of mind I drew near to that corner of the garden where she had stood with me, that quiet shady corner which henceforth would remain enshrined within my memory for her sake, which——

I stopped suddenly short at the sight of two figures—one in the cap and apron of a waiting-maid and the other in the gorgeous plush and gold braid of a footman; and they were standing upon the very spot where Lisbeth and I had stood, and in almost the exact attitude—it was desecration.

I stood stock-still despite the Imp's frantic tugs at my coat, all other feelings swallowed up in one of half-amused resentment. Then the resplendent footman happened to turn his head, presently espied me, and removing his plush-clad arm from the waist of the trim maid-servant, and doubling his fists, strode towards us with a truly terrible mien.

"And w'ot might your game be?" he inquired, with that supercilious air inseparable from plush and gold braid. "Oh, I know your kind, I do—I know yer!"

"Then, fellow," quoth I, "I know not thee."

"Don't get trying to come over me," said he indignantly. "The question is w'ot are you 'anging round 'ere for?"

Now, possibly deceived by my pacific attitude, or inspired by the bright eyes of the trim maid-servant, he seized me, none too gently, by the collar, to the horrified dismay of the Imp.

"Nay, but I will give thee monies——"

"You are a-going to come up to the 'ouse with me, and none of your nonsense, either; d'ye 'ear?"

"Then must I needs smite thee for a barbarious dog—hence—base slave—be-gone!"

Wherewith I delivered what is technically known in "sporting" circles as a "right hook to the ear," followed by a "left swing to the chin," and my assailant immediately disappeared behind a bush, with a flash of pink silk calves and buckled shoes. Then, while the trim maid-servant filled the air with her lamentations, the Imp and I ran hot-foot for the wall, over which I bundled him neck and crop, and we set off pell-mell along the river-path.

"Oh, Uncle Dick, he panted, "how—how fine you are! You knocked yon footman—

I mean varlet—from his saddle like—like anything. Oh, I do wish you would play like this every night!"

"Heaven forbid!" I exclaimed fervently.

Coming at last to the Shrubbery gate, we paused awhile to regain our breath.

"Uncle Dick," said the Imp, regarding me with a thoughtful eye, "did you see his arm—I mean before you smote him 'hip and thigh'?"

"I did."

"It was round her waist."

"Imp, it was."

"Just like Peter's?"

"Yes."

"An' the man with the funny name?"

"Archibald's, yes."

"An'—an'——"

"And mine," I put in, seeing he paused. 'Uncle Dick—why?"

"Ah! who knows, Imp—perhaps it was the Moon-magic. And now, by my troth! 'tis full time all good knights were snoring, so hey for bed and the Slumber-world!"

The ladder was dragged from its hiding-place, and the Imp, having mounted, watched me from his window as I returned it to the laurels for very obvious reasons.

"We didn't see any fairies, did we, Uncle Dick?"

"Well, I think I did, Imp, just for a moment; I may have been mistaken, of course; but anyhow, it has been a very wonderful night all the same. And so—fare thee well, fair Knight!"

CHAPTER V

THE EPISODE OF THE INDIAN'S AUNT

THE sun blazed down, as any truly self-respecting sun should, on a fine August afternoon; yet its heat was tempered by a soft, cool breeze that just stirred the leaves above my head.

The river was busy whispering many things to the reeds, things which, had I been wise enough to understand, might have helped me to write many wonderful books, for, as it is so very old, and has both seen and heard so much, it is naturally very wise. But alas! being ignorant of the language of rivers, I had to content myself with my own dreams, and the large, speckled frog that sat beside me, watching the flow of the river with his big, gold-rimmed eyes.

He was happy enough, I was sure. There was a complacent satisfaction in every line of his fat mottled body. And as I watched him my mind very naturally reverted to the *Pickwick Papers*, and I repeated Mrs. Leo Hunter's deathless ode, beginning:

> "Can I see thee panting, dying,
> On a log,
> Expiring frog!"

The big, green frog beside me listened with polite attention, but on the whole, seemed strangely unmoved. Remembering the book in my pocket, I took it out; an old book, with battered leathern covers, which has passed through many hands since it was first published, more than two hundred years ago.

Indeed it is a wonderful, a most delightful book, known to the world as *The Compleat Angler*, in which, to be sure, one may read something of fish and fishing, but more about old Izaak's lovable self, his sunny streams and shady pools, his buxom milkmaids, and sequestered inns, and his kindly animadversions upon men and things in general. Yet, as I say, he does occasionally speak of fish and fishing, and amongst other matters, concerning live frogs as bait, after describing the properest method of impaling one upon the hook, he ends with this injunction—

"Treat it as though you loved it, that it may live the longer!"

Up till now the frog had preserved his polite attentiveness in a manner highly creditable to his upbringing, but this proved too much; his overcharged feelings burst from him in a hoarse croak, and he disappeared into the river with a splash.

"Good afternoon, Uncle Dick!" said a voice at my elbow, and looking round, I beheld Dorothy. Beneath one arm she carried the fluffy kitten, and in the other hand a scrap of paper.

"I promised Reginald to give you this," she continued, "and—oh yes—I was to say 'Hist!' first."

"Really! And why were you to say 'Hist'?"

"Oh, because all Indians always say 'Hist!' you know."

"To be sure they do," I answered; "but am I to understand that you are an Indian?"

"Not to-day," replied Dorothy, shaking her head. "Last time Reginald painted me Auntie was awfull' angry—it took her and nurse ages to get it all off—the war-paint, I mean—so I'm afraid I can't be an Indian again!"

"That's very unfortunate!" I said.

"Yes, isn't it; but nobody can be an Indian chief without any war-paint, can they?"

"Certainly not," I answered. "You seem to know a great deal about it."

"Oh yes," nodded Dorothy. "Reginald has a book all about Indians and full of pictures—and here's the letter," she ended, and slipped it into my hand.

Smoothing out its many folds and creases, I read aloud, as follows:

"*To my pail-face brother:*

"'Ere another moon, Spotted Snaik will be upon the war-path, and red goar shall flo in buckkit-fulls."

"It sounds dreadful, doesn't it?" said Dorothy, hugging her kitten.

"Horrible!" I returned.

"He got it out of the book, you know," she went on, "but I put in the part about the buckets—a bucket holds such an awful lot, don't you think? But there's some more on the other page." Obediently I turned, and read:

"'ere another moon, scalps shall dangel at belt of Spotted Snaik, for in his futsteps lurks distruksion. But fear not pail-face, thou art my brother—fairwell.

"Sined

"SPOTTED SNAIK."

"There was lots more, and we couldn't get it in," said Dorothy. Squeezed up into a corner I found this postscript:

"If you will come and be an Indian Cheef unkel dick, I will make you a spear, and you can be Fanged Wolf. He was a fine chap and nobody could beat him except Spotted Snaik, will you Unkel dick?"

"He wants you to write an answer, and I'm to take it to him," said Dorothy.

"Fanged Wolf!" I repeated; "no, I'm afraid not. I shouldn't object so much to becoming a redskin—for a time—but Fanged Wolf! Really, Dorothy, I'm afraid I couldn't manage that."

"He was very brave," returned Dorothy, "and awfull' strong, and could—could 'throw his lance with such unerring aim as to pin his foe to the nearest tree—in the twinkle of an eye.' That's in the book, you know."

"There certainly must be a great deal of satisfaction in pinning one's foe to a tree," I nodded.

"Y-e-e-s, I suppose so," said Dorothy rather dubiously.

"And where is Spotted Snake—I mean, what is he doing?"

"Oh, he's down by the river, with his bow and arrow, scouting for canoes. It was great fun! He shot at a man in a boat—and nearly hit him, and the man got very angry indeed, so we had to hide among the bushes, just like real Indians. Oh, it was fine!"

"But your Auntie Lisbeth said you weren't to play near the river, you know," I said.

"That's what I told him," returned Dorothy, "but he said that Indians didn't have any aunts, and then I didn't know what to say. What do you think about it, Uncle Dick?"

"Well," I answered, "now I come to consider, I can't remember ever having heard of an Indian's aunt."

"Poor things!" said Dorothy, giving the fluffy kitten a kiss between the ears.

"Yes, it's hard on them, perhaps, and yet," I added thoughtfully, "an aunt is sometimes rather a mixed blessing. Still, whether an Indian possesses an aunt or not, the fact remains that water has an unpleasant habit of wetting one, and, on the whole, I think I'll go and see what Spotted Snake is up to."

"Then I think I'll come with you a little way," said Dorothy, as I rose. "You see, I have to get Louise her afternoon's milk."

"And how is Louise?" I inquired, pulling the fluffy kitten's nearest ear.

"Very well, thank you," answered Dorothy demurely; "but oh, dear me! kittens 'are such a constant source of worry and anxiety!' Auntie Lisbeth sometimes says that about Reginald and me. I wonder what she would say if we were kittens!"

"By the by, where is your Auntie Lisbeth?" I asked, in a strictly conversational tone.

"Well, she's lying in the old boat."

"In the old boat!" I repeated.

"Yes," nodded Dorothy; "when it's nice and warm and sleepy, like to-day, she takes a book, and a pillow, and a sunshade, and she goes and lies in the old boat under the water-stairs. There, just look at this naughty Louise!" she broke off, as the kitten scrambled up to her shoulder and stood there, balancing itself very dexterously with curious angular movements of its tail; "that's because she thinks I've forgotten her milk, you know; she's dreadfully impatient, but I suppose I must humour her this once. 'Good afternoon!'" And, having given me her hand in her demure, old-fashioned way, Dorothy hurried off, the kitten still perched upon her shoulder, its tail jerking spasmodically with her every step.

In a little while I came in view of the water-stairs, yet, although I paused more than once to look about me, I saw no sign of the Imp. Thinking he was most probably in "ambush" somewhere, I continued my way. whistling a tune to attract his notice. Ten minutes or more elapsed, however, without any sign of him, and I was already close to the stairs, when I stopped whistling all at once, and, holding my breath, crept forward on tiptoe.

There before me was the old boat, and in it—her cheek upon a crimson cushion and the sun making a glory of her tumbled hair—was Lisbeth—asleep.

Being come as near as I dared for fear of waking her, I sat down, and lighting my pipe, fell to watching her—the up-curving shadow of her lashes, the gleam of teeth between the scarlet of her parted lips. And from the heavy braids of her hair my glance wandered down to the little tan shoe peeping at me beneath her skirt, and I called to mind how Goethe has said:

"A pretty foot is not only a continual joy, but it is the one element of beauty that defies the assaults of Time."

Sometimes a butterfly hovered past, a bee filled the air with his drone, or a bird settled for a moment upon the stairs near by to preen a ruffled feather, while soft and drowsy with distance came the ceaseless roar of the weir.

I do not know how long I had sat thus,

supremely content, when I was suddenly aroused by a rustling close at hand.

"Hist!"

I looked up sharply, and beheld a head, a head adorned with sundry feathers, and a face hideously streaked with red and green paint; but there was no mistaking those golden curls—it was the Imp!

"Hist!" he repeated, bringing out the word with a prolonged hiss, and then— before I could even guess at his intention there was the swift gleam of a knife, a splash of the severed painter, and caught by the tide the old boat swung out and was adrift.

The Imp stood gazing on his handiwork with wide eyes, and then as I leaped to my feet something in my look seemed to frighten him, for, without a word, he turned and fled.

But all my attention was centred in the boat, which was drifting slowly into mid-stream with Lisbeth still fast asleep. And as I watched its sluggish progress, with a sudden chill I remembered the weir, which foamed and roared only a short half-mile away. If the boat once got drawn into that——!

Now, I am quite aware that under these circumstances the right and proper thing for me to have done would have been to throw aside my coat, tear off my boots, etc., and "boldly breast the foamy flood." But I did neither, for the simple reason that once within the "foamy flood" aforesaid, there would have been very little chance of my ever getting out again, for—let me confess the fact with the blush of shame—I am no swimmer.

Yet I was not idle, far otherwise. Having judged the distance between the drifting boat and the bank, I began running along, seeking the thing I wanted. And presently, sure enough I found it—a great pollard oak, growing upon the edge of the water, that identical tree with the "stickie-out" branches which has already figured in these narratives.

Hastily swinging myself up, I got astride the lowest branch, which projected out

over the water. I had distanced the
boat by some hundred yards, and as I
sat there I watched its drift, one minute
full of hope, and the next as miserably
uncertain.

My obvious intention was to crawl out
upon the branch until it bent with my weight,
and so let myself into, or as near the boat
as possible.

It was close now, so close that I could see
the gleam of Lisbeth's hair and the point
of the little tan shoe. With my eyes on
this, I writhed my way along the bough,
which bent more and more as I neared the
end. Here I hung, swaying up and down
and to and fro in a highly unpleasant manner,
while I waited the crucial moment.

Never upon this whole round earth did
anything creep as that boat did. There was
a majestic deliberation in its progress that
positively maddened me. I remember to
have once read an article somewhere upon
the "Sensibility of Material Things," or
something of the sort, which I had forgotten
long since, but as I hung there suspended

between heaven and earth, it came back
to me with a rush, and I was perfectly certain
that, recognising my precarious position, that
time-worn, ancient boat checked its speed
on purpose.

But all things have an end, and so, little
by little the blunt bow crept nearer until
it was in the very shade of my tree. Grasping
the branch, I let myself swing at arm's
length; and then I found that I was at least
a foot too near the bank. Edging my way,
therefore, still further along the branch, I
kicked out in a desperate endeavour to reach
the boat, and, the bough swaying with me,
caught my toe inside the gunwhale, drew
it under me, and loosing my grasp, was
sprawling upon my hands and knees, but
safe aboard.

To pick myself up was the work of a
moment, yet scarcely had I done so, when
Lisbeth opened her eyes, and sitting up.
stared about her.

"Why—where am I?" she exclaimed.

"On the river," I answered cheerfully.
"Glorious afternoon, Lisbeth, isn't it?"

"How—in—the—world did you get here?"
she inquired.

"Well," I answered, "I might say I
dropped in, as it were."

Lisbeth brushed the hair from her temples,
and turned to me with an imperious
gesture.

"Then please take me back at once," she
said.

"I would with pleasure," I returned,
"only that you forgot to bring the
oars."

"Why, then, we are adrift!" she said,
staring at me with frightened eyes, and
clasping her hands nervously.

"We are," I nodded; "but then, it's
perfect weather for boating, Lisbeth!" and
I began to look about for something that
might serve as a paddle. But the stretchers
had disappeared long since—the old tub
was a sheer hulk, so to speak. An attempt
to tear up a floor board resulted only in a
broken nail and bleeding fingers; so I
presently desisted, and, rolling up my
sleeves, endeavoured to paddle with my

hands; but, finding this equally futile, I resumed my coat, and took out pipe and tobacco.

"Oh, Dick, is there nothing you can do?" she asked, with a brave attempt to steady the quiver in her voice.

"With your permission, I'll smoke, Lisbeth."

"But the weir!" she cried. "Have you forgotten the weir?"

"No," I answered, shaking my head; "it has a way of obtruding itself on one's notice——"

"Oh, it sounds hateful—hateful!" she said with a shiver.

"Like a strong wind among trees!" I nodded, as I filled my pipe. We were approaching a part of the river where it makes a sharp bend to the right; and well I knew what lay beyond—the row of posts, painted white, with the foam and bubble of seething water below. We should round that bend in about ten minutes, I judged; long before then we might see a boat, to be sure; if not—well, if the worst happened, I could but do my best; in the meantime I would smoke a pipe; but I will admit my fingers trembled as I struck a match.

"It sounds horribly close!" said Lisbeth.

"Sound is very deceptive, you know," I answered.

"Only last month a boat went over, and the man was drowned!" shuddered Lisbeth.

"Poor chap!" I said "Of course it's different at night—the river is awfully deserted then, you know, and——"

"But it happened in broad daylight!" said Lisbeth, almost in a whisper. She was sitting half turned from me, her gaze fixed on the bend of the river, and by chance her restless hand had found and begun to fumble with the severed painter.

So we drifted on, watching the gliding banks, while every moment the roar of the weir grew louder and more threatening.

"Dick," she said suddenly, "we can never pass that awful place without oars! and she began to tie knots in the rope with fingers that shook pitifully.

"Oh, I don't know!" I returned, with an assumption of ease I was very far from feeling; "and then, of course, we are bound to meet a boat or something——"

"But suppose we don't?"

"Oh, well, we aren't there yet—and—er—let's talk of fish."

"Ah, Dick," she cried, "how can you treat the matter so lightly when we may be tossing down there in that awful water so very soon? We can never pass that weir without oars, and you know it, and—and—oh, Dick, why did you do it—how could you have been so mad?"

"Do what?" I inquired staring.

With a sudden gesture she rose to her knees and fronted me.

"This!" she cried, and held up the severed painter. "It has been cut! Oh, Dick, Dick, how could you be so mad?"

"Lisbeth!" I exclaimed, "do you mean to say that you think——"

"I know!" she broke in, and turning away, hid her face in her hands.

We were not so very far from the bend

now, and seeing this, a sudden inspiration came upon me, by means of which I might prove her mind towards me once and for all; and as she kneeled before me with averted face, I leaned forward and took her hands in mine.

"Lisbeth," I said, "supposing I did cut the boat adrift, like a—a fool—endangering your life for a mad, thoughtless whim— could you forgive me?"

For a long moment she remained without answering, then very slowly she raised her head.

"Oh, Dick!" was all she said, but in her eyes I read the wonder of wonders.

"But Lisbeth," I stammered, "could you still love me—even—even if, through my folly, the worst should happen and we— we——"

"I don't think I shall be so very much afraid, Dick, if you will hold me close like this," she whispered.

The voice of the weir had swelled into a roar by now, yet I paid little heed; for me, all fear was swallowed up in a great wondering happiness.

"Dick," she whispered, "you will hold me tight, you will not let me go when—when——"

"Never," I answered; "nothing could ever take you from me now."

As I spoke I raised my eyes, and glancing about beheld something which altered the whole aspect of affairs—something which changed tragedy into comedy all in a moment —a boat was coming slowly round the bend.

"Lisbeth, look up!" With a sigh she obeyed, her clasp tightening on mine, and a dreadful expectation in her eyes. Then all at once it was gone, her pale cheeks grew suddenly scarlet, and she slipped from my arms; and thereafter I noticed how very carefully her eyes avoided mine.

The boat came slowly into view, impelled by one who rowed with exactly that amount of splashing which speaks the true-born Cockney. By dint of much exertion and more splashing he presently ranged alongside in answer to my hail.

"W'ot—a haccident then?" he enquired.

"Something of the sort," I nodded. "Will you be so kind as to tow us to the bank yonder?"

"Hanythink to hoblige!" he grinned, and having made fast the painter, proceeded to splash us to *terra firma*. Which done, he grinned again, waved his hat, and splashed upon his way. I made the boat secure and turned to Lisbeth. She was staring away towards the weir.

"Lisbeth," I began.

"I thought just now that—that it was the end!" she said, and shivered.

"And at such times," I added, "one sometimes says things one would not have said under ordinary circumstances. My dear, I quite understand—quite, and I'll try to forget—you needn't fear."

"Do you think you can?" she asked, turning to look at me.

"I can but try," I answered. Now, as I spoke, I wasn't sure, but I thought I saw the pale ghost of the dimple by her mouth.

We walked back side by side along the river-path, very silently for the most part, yet more than once I caught her regarding me covertly, and with a puzzled air.

"Well?" I said at last tentatively.

"I was wondering why you did it, Dick. Oh, it was mean! cruel! wicked! How could you?"

"Oh, well"—and I shrugged my shoulders, anathematising the Imp mentally the while.

"If I hadn't noticed that the rope was freshly cut, I should have thought it an accident," she went on.

"Naturally!" I said.

"And then, again, how came you in the boat?"

"To be sure!" I nodded.

"Still, I can scarcely believe that you would wilfully jeopardise both our lives— my life!"

"A man who would do such a thing," I exclaimed, carried away by the heat of the moment, "would be a—a——"

"Yes," said Lisbeth quickly, "he would."

"—And utterly beyond the pale of all forgiveness!"

"Yes," said Lisbeth, "of course."

"And," I was beginning again, but meeting her searching glance, stopped. "And you forgave me, Lisbeth," I ended.

"Did I?" she said, with raised brows.

"Didn't you?"

"Not that I remember."

"In the boat?"

"I never *said* so."

"Not in words, perhaps, but you implied as much." Lisbeth had the grace to blush.

"Do I understand that I am not forgiven after all?"

"Not until I know why you did such a mad, thoughtless trick," she answered, with that determined set of her chin which I knew so well.

That I should thus shoulder the responsibility for the Imp's misdeeds was ridiculous, and wrong as it was unjust, for if ever boy deserved punishment, that boy was the Imp. And yet, probably because he was the Imp, or because of that schoolboy honour which forbids "sneaking," and which I carried with me still, I held my peace; seeing which, Lisbeth turned and left me.

I stood where I was, with head bent in an attitude suggestive of innocence, broken hopes, and gentle resignation, but in vain; she never once looked back. Still, martyr though I was, the knowledge that I had immolated myself upon the altar of friendship filled me with a sense of conscious virtue that I found not ill-pleasing. Howbeit, seeing I am but human after all, I sat down, and refilling my pipe, fell once more anathematising the Imp.

"Hist!"

A small shape flittered from behind an adjacent tree, and lo! the subject of my thoughts stood before me.

"Imp," I said, "come here." He obeyed readily. "When you cut that rope and set your Auntie Lisbeth adrift, you didn't remember the man who was drowned in the weir last month, did you?"

"No!" he answered, staring.

"Of course not," I nodded; "but all the same it is not your fault that your Auntie Lisbeth is not drowned—just as he was."

"Oh!" exclaimed the Imp, and his beloved bow slipped from his nerveless fingers.

"Imp," I went on, "it was a wicked thing to cut that rope, a mean, cruel trick. Don't you think so?"

"I 'specks it was, Uncle Dick."

"Don't you think you ought to be punished?" He nodded. "Very well," I answered, "I'll punish you myself. Go and cut me a nice, straight switch," and I handed him my open penknife. Round-eyed, the Imp obeyed, and for a space there was a prodigious cracking and snapping of sticks. In a little while he returned with three, also the blade of my knife was broken, for which he was profusely apologetic.

"Now," I said, as I selected the weapon fittest for the purpose, "I am going to strike you hard on either hand with this stick— that is, if you think you deserve it."

"Was Auntie Lisbeth nearly drowned—really?" he inquired.

"Very nearly, and was only saved by a chance."

"All right, Uncle Dick, hit me," he said, and held out his hand. The stick whizzed and fell—once—twice. I saw his face grow scarlet and the tears leap to his eyes, but he uttered no sound.

"Did it hurt very much, my Imp?" I inquired, as I tossed the stick aside.

He nodded, not trusting himself to speak, while I turned to light my pipe, wasting three matches quite fruitlessly.

"Uncle Dick," he burst out at last, struggling manfully against his sobs, "I—I'm awfull'—sorry——"

"Oh, it's all right now, Imp. Shake hands!" Joyfully the little, grimy fingers clasped mine, and from that moment, I think, there grew up between us a new understanding.

"Why, Imp, my darling, you're crying!" exclaimed a voice, and, with a rustle of skirts, Lisbeth was down before him on her knees.

"I know I am—'cause I'm awfull' sorry—an' Uncle Dick's whipped my hands—an' I'm glad!"

"Whipped your hands?" cried Lisbeth, clasping him closer, and glaring at me. "Whipped your hands? How dare he? What for?"

"'Cause I cut the rope an' let the boat go away with you an' you might have been drowned dead in the weir, an' I'm awfull' glad Uncle Dick whipped me!"

"O-h-h!" exclaimed Lisbeth, and it was a very long-drawn "oh!" indeed.

"I don't know what made me do it," continued the Imp. "I 'specks it was my new knife—it was so nice an' sharp, you know."

"Well, it's all right now, my Imp," I said, fumbling for a match in a singularly clumsy manner. "If you ask me, I think we are all better friends than ever—or should be. I know I should be fonder of your Auntie Lisbeth even than before, and take greater care of her, if I were you. And—now take her in to tea, my Imp, and

—and see that she has plenty to eat," and, lifting my hat, I turned away. But Lisbeth was beside me, and her hand was on my arm before I had gone a yard.

"We are having tea in the same old place—under the trees. If you would care to—to—would you?"

"Yes, do—oh, do, Uncle Dick!" cried the Imp. "I'll go and tell Jane to set a place for you," and he bounded off.

"I didn't hit him very hard," I said, breaking a somewhat awkward silence; "but, you see, there are some things a gentleman cannot do. I think he understands now."

"Oh, Dick!" she said very softly; "and to think I could imagine you had done such a thing—you! and to think that you should let me think you had done such a thing—and all to shield that Imp! Oh, Dick! no wonder he is so fond of you. He never talks of anyone but you—I grow quite jealous sometimes. But, Dick, how *did* you get into that boat?"

"By means of a tree with 'stickie-out' branches."

F

"Do you mean to say——"

"That, as I told you before, I dropped in, as it were."

"But supposing you had slipped?"

"But I didn't."

"And you can't swim a stroke!"

"Not that I know of."

"Oh, Dick! can you ever forgive me?"

"On three conditions."

"Well?"

"First, that you let me remember everything you said to me while we were drifting down to the weir."

"That depends, Dick. And the second?"

"The second lies in the fact that not far from the village of Down, in Kent, there stands an old house—a quaint old place that is badly in want of someone to live in it—an old house that is lonely for a woman's sweet presence and gentle, busy hands, Lisbeth!"

"And the third?" she asked very softly.

"Surely you can guess that?"

"No, I can't, and, besides, there's Dorothy coming—and—oh, Dick!"

"Why, Auntie," exclaimed Dorothy, as she came up, "how red you are! I knew you'd get sunburned, lying in that old boat without a parasol! But, then, she will do it, Uncle Dick—oh, she will do it!"

CHAPTER VI

THE OUTLAW

EVERYBODY knew old Jasper Trent, the Crimean veteran who helped to beat the "Roosians and the Proosians," and who, so it was rumoured had more wounds upon his worn, bent body than there were months in the year.

The whole village was proud of old Jasper, proud of his age, proud of his wounds, and proud of the medals that shone resplendent upon his shrunken breast.

Any day he might have been seen hobbling along by the river, or pottering among the flowers in his little garden, but oftener still sitting on the bench in the sunshine beside the door of the Three Jolly Anglers.

Indeed, they made a fitting pair, the worn old soldier and the ancient inn, alike both long behind the times, dreaming of the past, rather than the future, which seemed to me like an invisible bond between them. Thus, when old Jasper fell ill, and, taking to his bed, had it moved opposite the window where he could lie with his eyes upon the battered gables of the inn—I for one could understand the reason.

The Three Jolly Anglers is indeed ancient, its early records long since lost beneath the dust of centuries; yet the years have but served to mellow it. Men have lived and died, nations have waxed and waned, still it stands, all unchanged beside the river, watching the Great Tragedy which we call "Life" with the same look of supreme wisdom, that half-waggish, half-kindly air, which I have already mentioned once before.

Those Sons of the Soil, who meet regularly within its walls, are horny-handed, and for the most part grey of head and bent with over-much following of the plough. Quiet of voice are they, and profoundly sedate of gesture, while upon their wrinkled brows there sits that spirit of calm content which is given so few of us to know.

Chief among these, and held in much respect, was old Jasper Trent. Within their circle he had been wont to sit ensconced in his elbow-chair beside the hearth, by his long use and custom, and not to be usurped; and while the smoke rose slowly from their pipe-bowls he would recount some tale of battle and sudden death—now in the freezing trenches before Sebastopol, now upon the blood-stained heights of Inkerman. Yet, and I noticed it was always towards the end of his second tankard, the old man would lose the thread of his story, whatever it might be, and take up the topic of "The Bye Jarge."

I was at first naturally perplexed as to whom he could mean, until Mr. Amos Baggett, the landlord, informed me on the quiet that the "bye Jarge" was none other than old Jasper's only son—a man now some forty years of age—who, though promising well in his youth, had "gone wrong"—and was at that moment serving a long term of imprisonment for burglary; further, that upon the day of his son's conviction old Jasper had had a "stroke," and was never quite the same after, all recollection of the event being completely blotted from his mind, so that he persisted in thinking and speaking of his son as still a boy.

"That bye were a wonder!" he would say, looking round with a kindling eye. "Went away to make 'is fortun', 'e did. Oh, 'e were a gen'us, were that bye Jarge! You, Amos Baggett, were 'e a gen'us or were 'e not?"

"''E were!" Mr. Baggett would answer, with a slow nod.

"Look'ee, sir, do'ee see that theer clock?" —and he would point with a bony, tremulous finger — "stopped it were — got sum'mat wrong wi' its innards—wouldn't stir a finger —dead it were! But that bye Jarge 'e see it, 'e did—give it a look over, 'e did, an' wi' nout but 'is two 'ands set it a-going good as ever! You, Silas Madden. you remember as 'e done it wi' 'is two 'ands?"

"'Is two 'ands!" Silas would repeat solemnly.

"An' it's gone ever since!" old Jasper. would croak triumphantly. "Oh! 'e were a gen'us, were my bye Jarge. 'E'll come a-marching back to 'is old feyther, some day, wi' 'is pockets stuffed full o' money an' banknotes—I knaw—I knaw, old Jasper bean't a fule."

And herewith, lifting up his old, cracked voice, he would strike up "The British Grenadiers," in which the rest would presently join full lustily, waving their long-stemmed pipes in unison.

So the old fellow would sit, singing the praises of his scapegrace son, while his hearers would nod solemn heads, fostering old Jasper's innocent delusion for the sake of his white hairs and the medals upon his breast.

But now, he was down with "the rheumatics," and from what Lisbeth told me when I met her on her way to and from his cottage, it was rather more than likely that the high-backed elbow-chair would know him no more.

Upon the old fellow's illness, Lisbeth had promptly set herself to see that he was made comfortable, for Jasper was a lonely old man—had installed a competent nurse beside him, and made it a custom morning and evening to go and see that all was well.

It was for this reason that I sat upon the Shrubbery gate towards nine o'clock of a certain evening, swinging my legs and listening for the sound of her step along the path. In the fullness of time she came, and, getting off my perch, I took the heavy basket from her arm, as was usual.

"Dick," she said as we walked on side by side, "really I'm getting quite worried about that Imp."

"What has he been up to this time?" I inquired.

"I'm afraid he must be ill."

"He looked anything but ill yesterday," I answered reassuringly.

"Yes, I know he looks healthy enough," said Lisbeth, wrinkling her brows; "but lately he has developed such an enormous appetite. Oh, Dick, it's awful!"

"My poor girl," I retorted, shaking my head, "the genus 'Boy' is distinguished by the two attributes dirt and appetite. You should know that by this time. I myself have harrowing recollections of huge piles of bread and butter, of vast slabs of cake—damp and 'soggy,' and of mysterious hue—of glutinous mixtures purporting to be 'stick-jaw,' one inch of which was warranted to render coherent speech impossible for ten minutes at least. And then the joy of bolting things fiercely, in the shade of the pantry, with one's ears on the stretch for foes! I sometimes find myself sighing over the remembrance, even in these days. Don't worry about the Imp's appetite; believe me, it is quite unnecessary."

"Oh, but I can't help it," said Lisbeth; "it seems somehow so—so weird. For instance, this morning for breakfast he had first his usual porridge, then five pieces of bread and butter, and after that a large slice of ham—quite a big piece, Dick! And he ate it all so quickly. I turned away to ask Jane for the toast, and when I looked at his plate again it was empty, he had eaten every bit, and even asked for more. Of course I refused, so he tried to get Dorothy to give him hers in exchange for a broken pocket-knife. It was just the same at dinner. He ate the whole leg of a chicken, and after that a wing, and then some of the breast, and would have gone on until he had finished everything, I'm sure, if I hadn't stopped him, though I let him eat as long as I dared. Then at tea he had six slices of bread and butter, one after the other, not counting toast and cake. He has been like this for the last two days—and—oh yes, cook told me to-night that she found him actually eating dry bread just before he went up to bed. Dry bread—think of it! Oh, Dick, what can be the matter with him?"

"It certainly sounds mysterious," I answered, "especially as regards the dry bread; but that of itself suggests a theory, which, as the detective says in the story, 'I will not divulge just yet'; only don't worry, Lisbeth, the Imp is all right."

Being now come to old Jasper's cottage, which stands a little apart from the village in a bylane, Lisbeth paused and held out her hand for the basket.

"Don't wait for me to-night," she said. "I ordered Peter to fetch me in the dog-cart; you see, I may be late."

"Is the old chap so very ill?"

"Very, very ill, Dick."

"Poor old Jasper!" I exclaimed.

"Poor old Jasper!" she sighed, and her eyes were brimful of tenderness.

"He is very old and feeble," I said, drawing her close, under pretence of handing her the basket; "and yet, with your gentle hand to smooth my pillow, and your eyes to look into mine, I could almost wish——"

"Hush, Dick!"

"Peter or no Peter, I think I'll wait—unless you really wish me to say 'Good-night' now?" But with a dexterous turn she eluded me, and waving her hand hurried up the rose-bordered path.

An hour, or even two, does not seem so very long when one's mind is so full of happy thoughts as mine was. Thus, I was filling my pipe and looking philosophically about for a likely spot in which to keep my vigil, when I was aware of a rustling close by, and, as I watched, a small figure stepped from the shadow of the hedge out into the moonlight.

"Hallo, Uncle Dick!" said a voice.

"Imp!" I exclaimed; "what does this mean? You ought to have been in bed over an hour ago!"

"So I was," he answered, with his guileless smile; "only I got up again, you know."

"So it seems!" I nodded.

"An' I followed you an' Auntie Lisbeth all the way, too."

"Did you, though?"

"Yes, an' I dropped one of the parcels an' lost a sausage, but you never heard."

"Lost a sausage!" I repeated, staring.

"Oh, it's all right, you know," he hastened to assure me: "I found it again, an' it wasn't hurt a bit."

"Imp," I said sternly, "come here, I want to talk to you."

"Just a minute, Uncle Dick, while I get my parcels. I want you to help me tc carry them, please," and with the words he dived under the hedge, to emerge, a moment later, with his arms full of unwieldy packages, which he laid at my feet in a row.

"Why, what on earth have you got there, Imp?"

"This," he said, pointing to the first, "is jam an' ham an' a piece of bread; this next one is cakes an' sardines, an' this one is bread an' butter that I saved from my tea."

"Quite a collection!" I nodded. "Suppose you tell me what you mean to do with them."

"Well, they're for my outlaw. You remember the other day I wanted to play at being outlaws? Well, two days ago, as I was tracking a base caitiff through the woods with my trusty bow and arrow, I found a real outlaw in the old boat-house."

"Ah! and what is he like?" I inquired.

"Oh, just like an outlaw—only funny, you know, an' most awfull' hungry. Are all outlaws always so very hungry, Uncle Dick?"

"I believe they generally are, Imp. And he looks 'funny,' you say?"

"Yes; I mean his clothes are funny—all over marks like little crosses, only they aren't crosses."

"Like this?" I inquired; and picking up a piece of stick I drew a broad-arrow upon the path.

"Yes, just like that!" cried the Imp, in a tone of amazement. "How did you know? You're awfull' clever, Uncle Dick!"

"And he is in the old boat-house, is he?" I said, as I picked up an armful of packages. "'Lead on, Macduff!'"

"Mind that parcel, please, Uncle Dick; it's the one I dropped an' lost the sausage out of—there's one trying to escape now!"

Having reduced the recalcitrant sausage to a due sense of law and order, we proceeded toward the old boat-house—a dismal, dismantled affair, some half-mile or so down stream.

"And what sort of a fellow is your out-law, Imp?"

"Well, I 'spected he'd be awfull' fierce an' want to hold me for ransom, but he didn't; he's quite quiet, for an outlaw, with grey hair and big eyes, an' eats an awful lot."

"So you saved him your breakfast and dinner, did you?"

"Oh yes; an' my tea, too. Auntie Lisbeth got awfull' angry 'cause she said I ate too fast; an' Dorothy was frightened an' wouldn't sit by me 'cause she was 'fraid I'd burst—so frightfully silly of her!"

"By the way, you didn't tell me what you have there," I said, pointing to a huge, mis-shapen, newspaper parcel that he carried beneath one arm.

"Oh, it's a shirt, an' a coat, an' a pair of trousers of Peter's."

"Did Peter give them to you?"

"'Course not; I took them. You see, my outlaw got tired of being an outlaw, so he asked me to get him some 'togs,' meaning clothes, you know, so I went an' looked in the stable an' found these."

"You don't mean to say that you stole them, Imp?"

"'Course not!" he answered reproachfully. "I left Peter sixpence an' a note to say I would pay him for them when I got my pocket-money."

"Ah, to be sure!" I nodded.

We were close to the old boat-house now, and upon the Imp's earnest solicitations I handed over my bundles and hid behind a tree, because, as he pointed out, "his outlaw might not like me to see him just at first."

Having opened each package with great care and laid out their contents upon a log near by, the Imp approached the ruined building with signs of the most elaborate caution, and gave three loud, double knocks. Now casting my eyes about, I espied a short, heavy stick, and, picking it up, poised it in my hand ready in the event of possible contingencies.

The situation was decidedly unpleasant, I confess, for I expected nothing less than to be engaged in a desperate hand-to-hand struggle within the next few minutes; therefore I waited in some suspense, straining my eyes towards the shadows with my fingers clasped tight upon my bludgeon.

Then all at once I saw a shape, ghostly and undefined, flit swiftly from the gloom of the boat-house, and next moment a convict was standing beside the Imp, gaunt and tall and wild-looking in the moonlight.

His hideous clothes, stained with mud and the green slime of his hiding-places, hung upon him in tatters, and his eyes, deep-sunken in his pallid face, gleamed with an unnatural brightness as he glanced swiftly about him—a miserable, hunted creature, worn by fatigue and pinched with want and suffering.

"Did ye get 'em, sonny?" he inquired, in a hoarse, rasping voice.

"Ay, ay, comrade," returned the Imp; "all's well!"

"Bless ye for that, sonny!" he exclaimed, and with the words he fell to upon the food, devouring each morsel as it was handed to him with a frightful voracity, while his burning, restless eyes glared about him, never still for a moment.

Now as I noticed his wasted form and shaking limbs, I knew that I could master him with one hand. My weapon slipped from my slackened grasp, but at the sound, slight though it was, he turned and began to run. He had not gone five yards, however, when he tripped and fell, and before he could rise I was standing over him. He lay there at my feet, perfectly still, blinking up at me with red-rimmed eyes.

"All right, master," he said at last; "you've got me!"

But with the words he suddenly rolled himself towards the river, yet as he struggled to his knees I pinned him down again.

"Oh, sir, you won't go for to give me up to them?" he panted. "I've never done you no wrong. Don't send me back to it again, sir."

"'Course not," cried the Imp, laying his hand upon my arm; "this is only Uncle Dick. He won't hurt you; will you, Uncle Dick?"

"That depends," I answered, keeping tight hold of the tattered coat collar. "Tell me, what brings you hanging round here?"

"Used to live up in these parts once, master."

"Who are you?"

"Convict 49, as broke jail over a week ago an' would ha' died but for the little 'un there," and he nodded towards the Imp.

The convict, as I say, was a tall, thin fellow, with a cadaverous face lined with suffering, while the hair at his temples was prematurely white. And as I looked at him, it occurred to me that the suffering which had set its mark so deeply upon him was not altogether the grosser anguish of the body. Now for your criminal who can still feel morally there is surely hope. I think so, anyhow! For a long moment there was silence, while I stared into the haggard face below, and the Imp looked from one to the other of us, utterly at a loss.

"I wonder if you ever heard tell of 'the bye Jarge,'" I said suddenly.

The convict started so violently that the jacket tore in my grasp.

"How—how did ye know?" he gasped, and stared at me with dropped jaw.

"I think I know your father."

"My feyther," he muttered; "old Jasper —'e ain't dead, then?"

"Not yet," I answered; "come, get up, and I'll tell you more while you eat." Mechanically he obeyed, sitting with his glowing eyes fixed upon my face the while I told him of old Jasper's lapse of memory and present illness.

"Then 'e don't remember as I'm a thief an' convict 49, master?"

"No; he thinks and speaks of you always as a boy and a pattern son."

The man uttered a strange cry, and flinging himself upon his knees, buried his face in his hands.

"Come," I said, tapping him on the shoulder; "take off those things," and, nodding to the Imp, he immediately began unwrapping Peter's garments.

"What, master," cried the convict, starting up, "are you goin' to let me see 'im afore you give me up?"

"Yes," I nodded; "only be quick."

In less than five minutes the tattered prison dress was lying in the bed of the river, and we were making our way along the path towards old Jasper's cottage.

The convict spoke but once, and that as we reached the cottage gate:

"Is he very ill, sir?"

"Very ill," I said. He stood for a moment, inhaling the fragrance of the roses in great breaths, and staring about him; then with an abrupt gesture he opened the little gate, and gliding up the path with his furtive, stealthy footstep, he knocked at the door.

For some half-hour the Imp and I strolled to and fro in the moonlight, during which he related to me much about his outlaw and the many "ruses he had employed to get him provision." How upon one occasion, to escape the watchful eyes of Auntie Lisbeth, he had been compelled to hide a slice of jam tart in the trousers pockets, to the detriment of each; how Dorothy had watched him everywhere in the momentary

expectation of "something happening"; how
Jane and Peter and cook would stand and
stare and shake their heads at him because
he ate such a lot, "an' the worst of it was,
I was awfull' hungry all the time, you
know, Uncle Dick!" This and much more
he told me as we waited there in the moonlight.

At last the cottage door opened and the
convict came out. He did not join us at
once, but remained staring away towards
the river, though I saw him jerk his sieeve
across his eyes more than once in his furtive,
stealthy fashion, but when at last he came
up to us his face was firm and resolute.

"Did you see old Jasper?" I asked.

"Yes, sir, I saw him."

"Is he any better?"

"Much better—he died in my arms, sir.
An' now I'm ready to go back, there's a
police station in the village." He stopped
suddenly and turned to stare back at the
lighted windows of the cottage, and when
he spoke again his voice sounded hoarser
than ever.

"Thought I'd come back from furrin parts, 'e did, wi' my pockets stuffed full o' gold an' banknotes. Called me 'is bye Jarge, 'e did!" and again he brushed his cuff across his eyes.

"Master, I don't know who ye may be, but I'm grateful to ye an' more than grateful, sir. An' now I'm ready to go back an' finish my time."

"How much longer is that?"

"Three years, sir."

"And when you come out, what shall you do then?"

"Start all over again, sir; try to get some honest work an' live straight."

"Do you think you can?"

"I know I can, sir. Ye see, he died in my arms, called me 'is bye Jarge, said 'e were proud of me, 'e did! A man can begin again an' live straight an' square wi' a memory the like o' that to help him."

"Then why not begin to-night?"

He passed a tremulous hand through his silver hair, and stared at me with incredulous eyes.

"Begin—to-night," he half whispered.

"I have an old house among the Kentish hop gardens," I went on; "no one lives there at present except the caretaker, but it is within the bounds of probability that I may go to stay there—some day. Now the gardens need trimming, and I'm very fond of flowers. Do you suppose you could make the place look decent in—say, a month?"

"Sir," he said in a strange, broken voice, "you ain't jokin' with me, are you?"

"I could pay you a pound a week; what do you say?"

He tried to speak, but his lips quivered, and he turned his back upon us very suddenly. I tore a page from my pocket-book and scrawled a hasty note to my caretaker.

"Here is the address," I said, tapping him on the shoulder. "You will find no difficulty. I will write again to-night. You must, of course, have money to get there and may need to buy a few necessaries besides; here is your first week's wages in advance," and I thrust a sovereign into his hand. He stared down at it with blinking eyes, shuffling awkwardly with his feet, and at that moment his face seemed very worn, and lined, and his hair very grey, yet I had a feeling that I should not regret my quixotic action in the end.

"Sir," he faltered—"sir, do you mean ——?" and stopped.

"I mean that to-night 'the bye Jarge' has a chance to make a new beginning, a chance to become the man his father always thought he would be. Of course, I may be a fool to trust you. That only time will show; but, you see, I had a great respect for old Jasper. And, now that you have the address, you'd better go; stay, though, you must have a hat; folks might wonder—take this," and I handed him my cap.

"Sir, I can't thank ye now, I never can. It—it won't come; but——" With a nervous, awkward gesture he caught my hand, suddenly pressed it to his lips, and was gone down the lane.

Thus it was that old Jasper's "bye Jarge" went out to make a trial of life a second time, and as I watched him striding through the moonlight, his head erect, very different from the shambling creature he had been, it seemed to me that the felon was already ousted by the man.

" I 'specks he forgot all 'bout me," said the Imp disconsolately.

" No," I answered, shaking my head; " I don't think he will ever forget you, my Imp."

" I s'pose he's awfull' fond of you, Uncle Dick? "

" Not that I know of."

" Then why did he kiss your hand? "

" Oh, well—er—perhaps it is a way he has! "

" He didn't kiss mine," said the Imp.

A door opened and closed very softly, and Lisbeth came towards us down the path, whereupon the Imp immediately "took cover " in the ditch.

" He is dead, Dick! " she said, as I opened the gate. " He died in his son's arms— the George he was always talking about. And oh, Dick, he died trying to sing ' The British Grenadiers.' "

" Poor old Jasper! " I said.

" His son was a convict once, wasn't he? "

" Yes."

" It was strange that he should come back as he did—just in time; it almost seems like the hand of Providence, doesn't it, Dick? "

" Yes." Lisbeth was standing with her elbows upon the gate and her chin in her hands, staring up at the moon, and I saw that her eyes were wet with tears.

" Why, where is your cap? " she exclaimed when at last she condescended to look at me.

" On the head of an escaped convict," I answered.

" Do you mean——"

" The ' bye Jarge,' " I nodded.

" Oh, Dick! "

" Yes, Lisbeth; it was a ridiculous piece of sentiment, I admit. Your law-abiding, level-headed citizen would doubtless be highly shocked, not to say scandalised; likewise the Law might get up on its hind legs and kick—quite unpleasantly; but all the same, I did it."

" You were never what one might call —very ' level-headed,' were you, Dick? "

" No, I'm afraid not."

" And, do you know, I think that is the very reason why I—good gracious!—what is that? " She pointed toward the shadow of the hedge.

" Merely the Imp," I answered; " but never mind that—tell me what you were going to say—' the very reason why you '— what? "

" Reginald! " said Lisbeth, unheeding my question, " come here, sir! " Very sheepishly the Imp crept forth from the ditch, and coming up beside me, stole his hand into mine, and I put it in my pocket.

" Reginald," she repeated, looking from one to the other of us with that expression which always renews within me the memory of my boyish misdeeds, " why are you not asleep in bed? "

" 'Cause I had to go an' feed my outlaw, Auntie Lisbeth."

" And," I put in to create a diversion, " incidentally I've discovered the secret of his 'enormous appetite'. It is explained in three words, to wit, 'the bye Jarge.'"

"Do you mean to say——" began Lisbeth.

"Fed him regularly twice a day," I went on, "and nearly famished himself in the doing of it—you remember the dry-bread incident?"

"Imp!" cried Lisbeth; "Imp!" And she had him next moment in her arms.

"But Uncle Dick gave him a whole sovereign, you know," he began; "an'——"

"I sent him to a certain house, Lisbeth," I said, as her eyes met mine; "an old house that stands not far from the village of Down, in Kent, to prune the roses and things. I should like it to be looking its best when we get there; and——"

"An' my outlaw kissed Uncle Dick's hand," pursued the Imp. "Don't you think he must love him an awful lot?"

"I gave him a month to do it in," I went on; "but a month seems much too long when one comes to consider—what do you think, Lisbeth?"

"I think that I hear the wheels of the

dogcart!" she cried. Sure enough, a moment later Peter hove in view, and great was his astonishment at the sight of "Master Reginald."

"Peter," I said, "Miss Elizabeth has changed her mind, and will walk back with us; and—er—by the way, I understand that Master Reginald purchased a coat, a shirt, and a pair of trousers of you, for which he has already paid a deposit of sixpence. Now, if you will let me know their value——"

"That's hall right, Mr. Brent, sir. Betwixt you and me, sir, they wasn't up to much, no-how, the coat being tightish, sir —tightish—and the trousis uncommon short in the leg for a man o' my hinches, sir."

"Nevertheless," said I, "a coat's a coat, and a pair of trousers are indubitably a pair of trousers, and nothing can alter the fact; so if you will send me a bill some time, I shall be glad."

"Very good, Mr. Brent, sir." Saying which, Peter touched his hat, and turning, drove away.

"Now," I said, as I rejoined Lisbeth and the Imp, "I shall be glad if you will tell me how long it should take for my garden to look fair enough to welcome you?"

"Oh, well, it depends upon the gardener, and the weather, and—and heaps of things," she answered, flashing her dimple at me.

"On the contrary," I retorted, shaking my head, "it depends altogether upon the whim of the most beautiful, tempting——"

"Supposing," sighed Lisbeth, "supposing we talk of fish!"

"You haven't been fishing lately, Uncle Dick," put in the Imp.

"I've had no cause to," I answered; "you see, I am guilty of such things only when life assumes a grey monotony of hue and everything is a flat, dreary desolation. Do you understand, Imp?"

"Not 'zactly—but it sounds fine! Auntie Lisbeth," he said suddenly, as we passed at the Shrubbery gate, "don't you think my outlaw must be very, very fond of Uncle Dick to kiss his hand?"

"Why, of course he must," nodded Lisbeth.

"If," he went on thoughtfully, "if you love somebody—very much—would you kiss their hand, Auntie Lisbeth?"

"I don't know—of course not!"

"But why not—s'posing their hand was nice an' clean?"

"Oh, well—really, I don't know. Imp, run along to bed, do."

"You'll come and tuck me up, an' kiss me good-night, won't you?"

"To be sure I will," nodded Lisbeth.

"Why, then, I'll go," said the Imp; and with a wave of the hand to me he went.

"Dick," said Lisbeth, staring up at the moon, "it was very unwise of you, to say the least of it, to set a desperate criminal at large."

"I'm afraid it was, Lisbeth; but then I saw there was good in the fellow, you know, and—er——"

"Dick," she said again, and then laughed suddenly, with the dimple in full evidence, "you foolish old Dick—you know you would

G

have done it anyway for the sake of that old man."

"Poor old Jasper!" I said; "I'm really afraid I should." Then a wonderful thing happened; for as I reached out my hand to her, she caught it suddenly in hers, and before I knew, had pressed her lips upon it—and so was gone.

CHAPTER VII

THE BLASTED OAK

I HAD quarrelled with Lisbeth; had quarrelled beyond all hope of redemption and forgiveness, desperately, irrevocably, and it had all come about through a handkerchief—Mr. Selwyn's handkerchief.

At a casual glance this may appear all very absurd, not to say petty; but then I have frequently noticed that insignificant things very often serve for the foundation of great; and incidentally quite a surprising number of lives have been ruined by a handkerchief.

The circumstances were briefly these: In the first place, I had received the following letter from the Duchess, which had perturbed me not a little:

"MY DEAR DICK,—I hear that that Agatha Warburton creature has written threatening to cut off our dear Lisbeth with the proverbial shilling unless she complies with her wish and marries Mr. Selwyn within the year. Did you ever know of anything so disgusting?

"If I were Lisbeth, and possessed such a 'creature' for an aunt, I'd see her in Timbuctoo first—I would! But then, I forget the poor child has nothing in the world, and you little more, and 'love in a cottage' is all very well, Dick, up to a certain time. Of course, it is all right in novels, but you are neither of you in a novel, and that is the worst of it. If Providence had seen fit to make me Lisbeth's aunt, now, things might have been very different; but alas! it was not to be. Under the circumstances, the best thing you can do, for her sake and your own, is to turn your back upon Arcadia and try to forget it all as soon as possible in the swirl of London and everyday life.

Yours,

CHARLOTTE C.

"P.S.—Of course Romance is dead ages and ages ago; still, it really would be nice if you could manage to run off with her some fine night!"

Thus the fiat had gone forth, the time of waiting was accomplished; to-day Lisbeth must choose between Selwyn and myself.

This thought was in my mind as I strode along the river path, filling me with that strange exhilaration which comes, I suppose, to most of us when we face some climax in our lives.

But now the great question, How would she decide? leaped up and began to haunt me. Because a woman smiles upon a man, he is surely a most prodigious fool to flatter himself that she loves him, therefore. How would she decide? Nay, indeed; what choice had she between affluence and penury? Selwyn was wealthy and favoured by her aunt, Lady Warburton, while as for me, my case was altogether the reverse. And now I called to mind how Lisbeth had always avoided coming to any understanding with me, putting me off on one pretence or another, but always with infinite tact. So Fear came to me, and Doubt began to rear its head; my step grew slower and slower, till, reaching the Shrubbery gate, I leaned there in doubt whether to proceed or not. Summoning up my resolution, however, I went on, turning in the direction of the orchard, where I knew she often sat of a morning to read or make a pretence of sewing.

I had gone but a little way when I caught sight of two distant figures walking slowly across the lawn, and recognised Lisbeth and Mr. Selwyn.

The sight of him here at such a time was decidedly unpleasant, and I hurried on, wondering what could have brought him so early.

Beneath Lisbeth's favourite tree, an ancient apple-tree so gnarled and rugged that it seemed to have spent all its days tying itself into all manner of impossible knots—in the shade of this tree, I say, there was a rustic seat and table, upon which was a work-basket, a book, and a handkerchief. It was a large, decidedly masculine handkerchief, and as my eyes encountered it, by some unfortunate chance I noticed a monogram embroidered in one corner—an extremely neat, precise monogram, with the letters "F.S." I recognised it at once as the property of Mr. Selwyn.

Ordinarily I should have thought nothing of it, but to-day it was different; for there are times in one's life when the most foolish things become pregnant of infinite possibilities; when the veriest trifles assume overwhelming proportions, filling and blotting out the universe.

So it was now, and as I stared down at the handkerchief, the Doubt within me grew suddenly into Certainty.

I was pacing restlessly up and down when I saw Lisbeth approaching; her cheeks seemed more flushed than usual, and her hand trembled as she gave it to me.

"Why, whatever is the matter with you?" she said; "you look so—so strange, Dick."

"I received a letter from the Duchess this morning."

"Did you?"

"Yes; in which she tells me your Aunt has threatened to——"

"Cut me off with a shilling," nodded Lisbeth, crossing over to the table.

"Yes," I said again.

"Well?"

"Well?"

"Oh, for goodness' sake, Dick, stop tramping up and down like a—a caged bear, and sit down—do!"

I obeyed; yet as I did so I saw her with the tail of my eye whip up the handkerchief and tuck it beneath the laces at her bosom.

"Lisbeth," said I, without turning my head, "why hide it—there?"

Her face flushed painfully, her lips quivered, and for a moment she could find no answer; then she tried to laugh it off.

"Because I—I wanted to, I suppose."

"Obviously!" I retorted, and, rising, bowed and turned to go.

"Stay a moment, Dick. I have something to tell you."

"Thank you, but I think I can guess."

"Can you?"

"Oh yes."

"Aren't you just a little bit theatrical, Dick?" Now, as she spoke she drew out Selwyn's handkerchief and began to tie and untie knots in it.

"Dick," she went on—and now she was tracing out Selwyn's monogram with her finger—"you tell me you know that Aunt Agatha has threatened to disinherit me; can you realise what that would mean to me, I wonder?"

"Only in some small part," I answered bitterly; "but it would be awful for you, of course—good-bye to society and all the rest of it—no more ball-gowns or hats and things from Paris, and——"

"And bearing all this in mind," she put in, "and knowing me as you do, perhaps you can make another guess and tell me what I am likely to do under these circumstances?"

Now, had I been anything but a preposterous ass, my answer would have been different; but then I was not myself, and

I could not help noticing how tenderly her finger traced out those two letters "F. S.," so I laughed rather brutally and answered—

"Follow the instinct of your sex and stick to the Paris hats and things."

I heard her breath catch, and turning away, she began to flutter the pages of the book upon the table.

"And you were always so clever at guessing, weren't you?" she said after a moment, keeping her face averted.

"At least it has saved your explaining the situation, and you should be thankful for that."

The book slipped suddenly to the ground and lay, all unheeded, and she began to laugh in a strange high key. Wondering, I took a step toward her; but as I did so she fled from me, running toward the house, never stopping or slackening speed, until I had lost sight of her altogether.

Thus the whole miserable business had befallen, dazing me by its very suddenness like a "bolt from the blue." I had returned to the Three Jolly Anglers, determined to follow the advice of the Duchess and return to London by the next train. Yet, after passing a sleepless night, here I was sitting in my old place beneath the alders pretending to fish.

The river was laughing among the reeds just as merrily as ever, bees hummed and butterflies wheeled and hovered—life and the world were very fair. Yet for once I was blind to it all; moreover, my pipe refused to "draw"—pieces of grass, twigs, and my penknife were alike unavailing.

So I sat there, brooding upon the fickleness of womankind, as many another has done before me, and many will doubtless do after, alack!

And the sum of my thoughts was this: Lisbeth had deceived me; the hour of trial had found her weak; my idol was only common clay, after all. And yet she had but preferred wealth to comparative poverty, which surely, according to all the rules of common sense, had shown her possessed of a wisdom beyond her years. And who was I to sit and grieve over it? Under the same circumstances ninety-nine women out of a hundred would have chosen precisely the same course; but then to me Lisbeth had always seemed the one exempt—the hundredth woman; moreover, there be times when love, unreasoning and illogical, is infinitely more beautiful than this much-vaunted common sense.

This and much more was in my mind as I sat fumbling with my useless pipe and staring with unseeing eyes at the flow of the river. My thoughts, however, were presently interrupted by something soft rubbing against me, and looking down, I beheld Dorothy's fluffy kitten, Louise. Upon my attempting to pick her up, she bounded from me in that remarkable sideways fashion peculiar to her kind, and stood regarding me from a distance, her tail straight up in the air and her mouth opening and shutting without a sound. At length, having given vent to a very feeble attempt at a mew, she zig-zagged to me, and, climbing upon my knee, immediately fell into a purring slumber.

"Hallo, Uncle Dick!—I mean, what ho, Little-John!" cried a voice, and looking over my shoulder carefully, so as not to disturb the balance of "Louise," I beheld the Imp. It needed but a glance at the bow in his hand, the three arrows in his belt, and the feather in his cap, to tell me who he was for the time being.

"How now, Robin?" I inquired.

"I'm a bitter, disappointed man, Uncle Dick!" he answered, putting up a hand to feel if his feather was in place.

"Are you?"

"Yes; the book says that Robin Hood was 'bitter an' disappointed,' an' so am I!"

"Why, how's that?"

The Imp folded his arms and regarded me with a terrible frown.

"It's all the fault of my Auntie Lisbeth!" he said in a tragic voice.

"Sit down, my Imp, and tell me all about it."

"Well," he began, laying aside his "trusty sword," and seating himself at my elbow, "she got awfull' angry with me yesterday, awfull' angry, indeed, and she wouldn't play with me or anything; an' when I tried to be friends with her an' asked her to pretend she was a hippopotamus, 'cause I was a mighty hunter, you know, she just said, 'Reginald, go away an' don't bother me!'"

"You surprise me, Imp!"

"But that's not the worst of it," he continued, shaking his head gloomily; "she didn't come to 'tuck me up' an' kiss me good-night like she always does. I lay awake hours an' hours waiting for her, you know; but she never came, an' so I've left her!"

"Left her!" I repeated.

"For ever an' ever!" he said, nodding a stern brow. "I 'specks she'll be awfull' sorry some day."

"But where shall you go to?"

"I'm thinking of Persia!" he said darkly.

"Oh!"

"It's nice an' far, you know, an' I might meet Aladdin with the wonderful lamp."

"Alas, Imp, I fear not," I answered, shaking my head; "and besides, it will take a long, long time to get there, and where shall you sleep at night?"

The Imp frowned harder than ever, staring straight before him as one who wrestles with some mighty problem; then his brow cleared and he spoke in this wise:

"Henceforth, Uncle Dick, my roof shall be the broad expanse of heaven, an'—an'— wait a minute!" he broke off, and, lugging something from his pocket, disclosed a tattered, paper-covered volume (the Imp's books are always tattered), and hastily turning the pages, paused at a certain paragraph and read as follows:

"'Henceforth my roof shall be the broad expanse of heaven, an' all tyrants shall learn to tremble at my name!' Doesn't that sound fine, Uncle Dick? I tried to get Ben—you know, the gardener's boy— to come an' live in the 'greenwood' with me a bit and help to make 'tyrants' tremble, but he said he was 'fraid his mother might find him some day, an' he wouldn't, so

I'm going to make them tremble all by myself, unless you will come an' be Little-John, like you were once before—oh do!"

Before I could answer, hearing footsteps, I looked round, and my heart leaped, for there was Lisbeth coming down the path.

Her head was drooping, and she walked with a listless air. Now, as I watched I forgot everything but that she looked sad, and troubled, and more beautiful than ever, and that I loved her. Instinctively I rose, lifting my cap. She started, and for the fraction of a second her eyes looked into mine, then she passed serenely on her way. I might have been a stick or stone for all the further notice she bestowed.

Side by side, the Imp and I watched her go, until the last gleam of her white skirt had vanished amid the green. Then he folded his arms and turned to me.

"So be it!" he said, with an air of stern finality; "an' now, what is a 'blasted oak,' please?"

"A blasted oak?" I repeated.

"If you please, Uncle Dick."

"Well, it's an oak-tree that has been struck by lightning."

"Like the one with the 'stickie-out' branches where I once hid Auntie Lis—Her stockings?"

I nodded, and, sitting down, began to pack up my fishing rod and things.

"I'm glad of that," pursued the Imp thoughtfully. "Robin Hood was always saying to somebody, 'Hie thee to the blasted oak at midnight!' an' it's nice to have one handy, you know."

I only said "Yes," and sighed.

"'Whence that doleful visage,' Uncle Dick—I mean, Little-John? Is Auntie angry with you, too?"

"Yes," I answered, and sighed again.

"Oh!" said the Imp, staring, "an' do you feel like—like—wait a minute"—and once more he drew out and consulted the tattered volume—"'do you feel like hanging yourself in your sword-belt to the arm of yonder tree?'" he asked eagerly, with his finger upon a certain paragraph.

"Very like it, my Imp."

"Or—or 'hurling yourself from the top-most pinnacle of yon lofty crag?'"

"Yes, Imp; the 'loftier' the better."

"Then you must be in love, like Alan-a-Dale; he was going to hang himself, an' 'hurl himself off the topmost pinnacle,' you know, only Robin Hood said, 'Whence that doleful visage?' an' stopped him—you remember?"

"To be sure," I nodded.

"An' so you are really in love with **my** Auntie Lis—Her, are you?"

"Yes."

"Is that why she's angry with you?"

"Probably."

The Imp was silent, apparently plunged once more in a profound meditation.

"'Fraid there's something wrong with her," he said at last, shaking his head; "she's always getting angry with everybody 'bout something—you an' me an' Mr. Selwyn——"

"Mr. Selwyn!" I exclaimed. "Imp, what do you mean?"

"Well, she got cross with me first—

an' over such a little thing too! We were
in the orchard, an' I spilt some lemonade
on her gown—only about half a glass, you
know, an' when she went to wipe it off
she hadn't a handkerchief, an' 'course I
had none. So she told me to fetch one,
an' I was just going when Mr. Selwyn came,
so I said, 'Would he lend Auntie Lisbeth
his handkerchief, 'cause she wanted one
to wipe her dress?' and he said 'Delighted!'
Then Auntie frowned at me an' shook her
head when he wasn't looking. But Mr. Selwyn
took out his handkerchief, an' got down on his
knees, an' began to wipe off the lemonade,
telling her something 'bout his 'heart,' an'
wishing he could 'kneel at her feet for ever'!
Auntie got awfull' red, and told him to stand
up, but he wouldn't; an' then she looked at
me so awfull' cross that I thought I'd better
leave, so while she was saying, 'Rise, Mr.
Selwyn—do!' I ran away, only I could
tell she was awfull' angry with Mr. Selwyn—
an' that's all!"

I rose to my knees, and caught the Imp
by the shoulders.

"Imp," I cried, "are you sure—quite sure that she was angry with Mr. Selwyn yesterday morning?"

"'Course I am. I always know when Auntie Lisbeth's angry. An' now let's go an' play at 'Blasted Oaks.'"

"Anything you like, Imp, so long as we find her."

"You're forgetting your fishing-rod an'——"

"Bother the fishing-rod!" I exclaimed, and set off hurriedly in the direction Lisbeth had taken.

The Imp trotted beside me, stumbling frequently over his "trusty sword" and issuing numberless commands in a hoarse, fierce voice to an imaginary "band of outlaws." As for me, I strode on unheeding, for my mind was filled with a fast-growing suspicion that I had judged Lisbeth like a hasty fool.

In this manner we scoured the neighbourhood very thoroughly, but with no success. However, we continued our search with unabated ardour—along the river path

to the water-stairs and from thence by way
of the gardens to the orchard; but not a
sign of Lisbeth. The shrubbery and paddock yielded a like result, and having
interrogated Peter in the harness-room,
he informed us that "Miss Helezabeth was
hout along with Miss Dorothy."

At last, after more than an hour of this
sort of thing, even the Imp grew discouraged
and suggested "turning pirates."

Our wanderings had led by devious paths,
and now, as luck would have it, we found
ourselves beneath "the blasted oak."

We sat down very solemnly side by side,
and for a long time there was silence.

"It's fine to make 'tyrants tremble,'
isn't it, Uncle Dick?" said the Imp at
last.

"Assuredly," I nodded.

"But I should have liked to kiss Auntie
Lisbeth good-bye first, an' Dorothy an'
Louise——"

"What do you mean, my Imp?"

"Oh, you know, Uncle Dick! 'My roof
henceforth shall be the broad expanse.' I'm

going to fight giants an'—an' all sorts of cads, you know. An' then, if ever I get to Persia an' do find the wonderful lamp, I can wish everything all right again, an' we should all be 'happy ever after'—you an' Auntie Lisbeth an' Dorothy an' me; an' we could live in a palace with slaves. Oh, it would be fine!"

"Yes, it's an excellent idea, Imp, but on the whole slightly risky, because it's just possible that you might never find the lamp; besides, you'll have to stop here, after all, because, you see, I'm going away myself."

"Then let's go away together, Uncle Dick, do!"

"Impossible, my Imp; who will look after your Auntie Lisbeth and Dorothy and Louise?"

"I forgot that," he answered ruefully.

"And they need a deal of taking care of," I added.

"'Fraid they do," he nodded; "but there's Peter," he suggested, brightening.

"Peter certainly knows how to look after

horses, but that is not quite the same. Lend me your 'trusty sword.'"

He rose, and drawing it from his belt, handed it to me with a flourish.

"You remember in the old times, Imp, when knights rode out to battle, it was customary for them when they made a solemn promise to kiss the cross-hilt of their swords, just to show they meant to keep it. So now I ask you to go back to your Auntie Lisbeth, to take care of her, to shield and guard her from all things evil, and never to forget that you are her loyal and true knight; and now kiss your sword in token, will you?" and I passed back the weapon.

"Yes," he answered, with glistening eyes, "I will, on my honour," and he kissed the sword.

"Good!" I exclaimed. "Thank you, Imp."

"But are you really going away?" he inquired, looking at me with a troubled face.

"Yes!"

"Must you go?"

"Yes."

"Will you promise to come back some day—soon?"

"Yes, I promise."

"On your honour?"

"On my honour!" I repeated, and in my turn I obediently kissed his extended sword-hilt.

"Are you going to-night, Uncle Dick?"

"I start very early in the morning, so you see we had better say 'good-bye' now, my Imp."

"Oh!" he said, and stared away down the river. Now, in the buttonhole of my coat there hung a fading rosebud which Lisbeth had given me two days ago, and acting on impulse, I took it out.

"Imp," I said, "when you get back, I want you to give this to your Auntie Lisbeth and say—er—never mind, just give it to her, will you?"

"Yes, Uncle Dick," he said, taking it from me, but keeping his face turned away.

"And now good-bye, Imp!"

"Good-bye!" he answered, still without looking at me.

"Won't you shake hands?"

He thrust out a grimy little palm, and as I clasped it I saw a big tear roll down his cheek.

"You'll come back soon—very soon—Uncle Dick?"

"Yes, I'll come back, my Imp."

And thus it was we parted, the Imp and I, beneath the "blasted oak," and I know my heart was strangely heavy as I turned away and left him.

After I had gone some distance I paused to look back. He still stood where I had left him, but his face was hidden in his arms as he leaned sobbing against the twisted trunk of the great tree.

All the way to the Three Jolly Anglers and during the rest of the evening the thought of the little desolate figure haunted me, so much so that, having sent away my dinner untasted, I took pen and ink and wrote him a letter, enclosing with it my penknife, which I had often seen him regard with "the eye of desire," despite the blade he had broken upon a certain memorable occasion. This done, I became possessed of a determination to send some message to Lisbeth also—just a few brief words which should yet reveal to her something of the thoughts I bore her ere I passed out of her life for ever.

For over an hour I sat there, chewing the stem of my useless pipe and racking my brain, but the "few brief words" obstinately refused to come.

Nine o'clock chimed mournfully from the Norman tower of the church hard by, yet still my pen was idle and the paper before me blank; also I became conscious of a tapping somewhere close at hand, now stopping, now beginning again, whose wearisome iteration so irritated my fractious nerves that I flung down my pen and rose.

The noise seemed to come from the vicinity of the window. Crossing to it, therefore, I flung the casement suddenly open, and found myself staring into a round face, in which were set two very round eyes and a button of a nose, the whole surmounted by a shock of red hair.

"'Allo, Mr. Uncle Dick!"

It needed but this and a second glance at the round face to assure me that it pertained to Ben, the gardener's boy.

"What, my noble Benjamin?" I exclaimed.

"No, it's me!" answered the redoubtable Ben. "'E said I was to give you this an' tell you, 'Life an' death!'" As he spoke he held out a roll of paper tied about the middle with a boot lace; which done, the round head grinned, nodded, and disappeared from my ken. Unwinding the boot lace I spread out the paper and read the following words, scrawled in pencil:

"Hi the to the Blarsted Oke and all will be forgiven. Come back to your luving frends and bigones shall be bigones. Look to the hole in the trunk there of.

      "Sined,

        "ROBIN, Outlaw and Knight.

"P.S.—I mean where i hid her stockings—you no."

I stood for some time with this truly mysterious document in my hand, in two minds what to do about it; if I went, the chances were that I should run against the Imp, and there would be a second leave-taking, which in my present mood I had small taste for. On the other hand, there was a possibility that something might have transpired which I should do well to know.

And yet what more could transpire? Lisbeth had made her choice, my dream was over, to-morrow I should return to London —and there was an end of it all; still——

In this pitiful state of vacillation I remained for some time, but in the end curiosity and a fugitive hope gained the day, and, taking my cap, I sallied forth.

It was, as Stevenson would say, "a wonderful night of stars," and the air was full of their soft, quivering light, for the moon was late and had not risen as yet. As I stepped

from the inn door, somebody in the tap-
room struck up "Tom Bowling" in a rough
but not unmusical voice; and the plaintive
melody seemed somehow to become part
of the night.

Truly my feet trod a path of "faerie,"
carpeted with soft mosses, a path winding
along beside a river of shadows, on whose
dark tide stars were floating. I walked
slowly, breathing the fragrance of the night
and watching the great silver moon creeping
slowly up the spangled sky. So I presently
came to the "blasted oak." The hole in
the trunk needed little searching for. I
remembered it well enough, and thrusting
in my hand, drew out a folded paper. Holding this close to my eyes, I managed with
no little difficulty to decipher this message:

"Don't go unkel dick bekors Auntie lisbeth wants you and i want you to. I heard
her say so to herself in the libree and she
was crying to, and didn't see me there but i
was. And she said O Dick i want you

so, out loud bekors she didn't no I was there. And i no she was crying bekors i saw the tiers. And this is true on my onner.

> "Sined,
> "Yore true frend and Knight,
> "REGINALD AUGUSTUS."

A revulsion of feeling swept over me as I read. Ah! if only I could believe she had said such words—my beautiful, proud Lisbeth.

Alas! dear Imp, how was it possible to believe you? And because I knew it could not possibly be true, and because I would have given my life to know that it was true, I began to read the note all over again.

Suddenly I started and looked round; surely that was a sob! But the moon's level rays served only to show the utter loneliness about me. It was imagination, of course, and yet it had sounded very real.

And she said, "Oh, Dick, I want you so!"

The river lapped softly against the bank, and somewhere above my head the leaves rustled dismally.

"Dear little Imp, if it were only true!"

Once again the sound came to me, low and restrained, but a sob unmistakably.

On the other side of the giant tree I beheld a figure half-sitting, half lying. The shadow was deep here, but as I stooped the kindly moon sent down a shaft of silver light, and I saw a lovely, startled face, with great, tear-dimmed eyes.

"Lisbeth!" I exclaimed; then, prompted by a sudden thought, I glanced hastily around.

"I am alone," she said, interpreting my thought aright.

"But—here—and—and at such an hour!" I stammered foolishly. She seemed to be upon her feet in one movement, fronting me with flashing eyes.

"I came to look for the Imp. I found this on his pillow. Perhaps you will explain?" and she handed me a crumpled paper.

"DEAR AUNTIE LISBATH" (I read)—"Unkel dick is going away bekors he is in luv with you and you are angry with him. Will you come at nine o'clock to the Blarsted oke, where I hid yore stokkings if you want to kiss me and be kind to me again, come to me bekors I want somebboddie to be nice to me now he is gone.

"yore luving sorry Imp.

"P.S.—He said he would like to hang himself in his sword-belt to the arm of yonder tree and hurl himself from yon topmost pinnakel, so I know he is in luv with you."

"Oh, blessed Imp!"

"And now where is he?" she demanded.

"Lisbeth, I don't know."

"You don't know! Then why are you here?"

For answer I held out the letter I had found, and watched while she read the words I could not believe.

Her hat was off, and the moon made wonderful lights in the coils of her black hair. She was wearing an indoor gown of some thin material that clung, revealing the gracious lines of her supple figure, and in the magic of the moon she seemed some young goddess of the woods—tall and fair and strong, yet infinitely womanly.

Now as she finished reading she turned suddenly away, yet not before I had seen the tell-tale colour glowing in her cheeks—a slow wave which surged over her from brow to chin, and chin to the round, white column of her throat.

"And she said, 'Oh, Dick, I want you so!'" I read aloud.

"Oh," Lisbeth murmured.

"Lisbeth, is it true?"

She stood with face averted, twisting the letter in her fingers.

"Lisbeth!" I said, and took a step nearer. Still she did not speak, but her hands came out to me with a swift, passionate gesture, and her eyes looked into mine; and surely none were ever more sweet, with the new shyness in their depths and the tears glistening on their lashes.

H

And in that moment Doubt and Fear were swallowed up in a great joy, and I forgot all things save that Lisbeth was before me and that I loved her.

The moon, risen now, had made a broad path of silver across the shadowy river to our very feet, and I remembered how the Imp had once told me that it was there for the moon fairies to come down by when they bring us happy dreams. Surely, the air was full of moon fairies to-night.

"Oh, Imp, thrice blessed Imp!"

"But—but Selwyn?" I groaned at last.

"Well?"

"If you love him——"

"But I don't!"

"But if you are to marry him——"

"But I'm not. I was going to tell you so in the orchard yesterday, but you gave me no chance; you preferred to guess, and, of course, guessed wrong altogether. I knew it made you wretched, and I was glad of it, and meant to keep you so a long, long time; but when I looked up and saw you standing there so very, very miserable, Dick, I couldn't keep it up any longer, because I was so dreadfully wretched myself, you know."

"Can you ever forgive me?"

"That depends, Dick."

"On what?"

Lisbeth stooped, and, picking up her hat, began to put it on.

"Depends on what?" I repeated.

Her hat was on now, but for a while she did not answer, her eyes upon the "fairy path." When at last she spoke her voice was very low and tender.

"'Not far from the village of Down, in Kent, there is a house,'" she began, "'a very old house, with pointed gables and panelled chambers, but empty to-night and desolate.' You see I remember it all," she broke off.

"Yes, you remember it all," I repeated, wondering.

"Dick—I—I want you to—take me there. I've thought of it all so often. Take me there, Dick."

"Lisbeth, do you mean it?"

"It has been the dream of my life for a long time now—to work for you there, to take care of you, Dick—you need such a deal, such a great deal of taking care of—to walk with you in the old rose garden; but I'm a beggar now, you know, though I shan't mind a bit if—if you want me, Dick."

"Want you?" I cried, and with the words I drew her close and kissed her.

Now, from somewhere in the tree above came a sudden crack and mighty snapping of twigs.

"All right, Uncle Dick!" cried a voice; "it's only the branch. Don't worry."

"Imp!" I exclaimed.

"I'm coming, Uncle Dick," he answered, and with much exertion and heavy breathing he presently emerged into view and squirmed himself safely to earth. For a moment he stood looking from one to the other of us, then he turned to Lisbeth.

"Won't you forgive me, too, Auntie Lisbeth, please?" he said.

"Forgive you?" she cried, and, falling on her knees, gathered him in her arms.

"I'm glad I didn't go to Persia, after all, Uncle Dick," he said over her shoulder.

"Persia?" repeated Lisbeth wonderingly.

"Oh, yes; you were so angry with Uncle Dick and me—so frightfull' angry, you know, that I was going to try to find the 'wonderful lamp' so I could wish everything all right again an' all of us 'live happy ever after'; but the blasted oak did just as well, an' was nicer, somehow, wasn't it?"

"Infinitely nicer," I answered.

"An' you will never be angry with Uncle Dick or me any more, will you, Auntie—that is, not frightfull' angry, you know?"

"Never any more, dear."

"On your honour?"

"On my honour!" she repeated, smiling, but there were tears in her voice.

Very gravely the Imp drew his "trusty word," which she, following his instructions, obediently kissed.

"And now," cried he, "we are all happy again, aren't we?"

"More happy than I ever hoped or dreamed to be," answered Lisbeth, still upon her knees; "and oh, Imp—dear little Imp, come and kiss me."

CHAPTER VIII

THE LAND OF HEART'S DELIGHT

SURELY there never was and never could be such another morning as this? Ever since the first peep of dawn a blackbird had been singing to me from the fragrant syringa-bush that blossomed just beneath my window. Each morning I had wakened to the joyous melody of his golden song. But to-day the order was reversed. I had sat there at my open casement, breathing the sweet purity of the morning, watching the eastern sky turn slowly from pearl-grey to saffron and from saffron to deepest crimson, until at last the new-risen sun had filled all the world with his glory. And then this blackbird of mine had begun—very hoarse at first, trying a note now and then in a tentative sort of fashion, as though still drowsy and not quite sure of himself, but little by little his notes had grown longer, richer, mellower, until here he was pouring out his soul in an ecstasy.

Ah! surely there never was, there never could be, such another morning as this!

Out of the green twilight of the woods a gentle wind was blowing, laden with the scent of earth and hidden flowers. Dewdrops twinkled in the grass and hung glistening from every leaf and twig, and beyond all was the sheen of the murmurous river.

The blackbird was in full song now, and by degrees others joined in—thrush, and lark, and linnet, with the humbler voices of the farmyard—until the sunny air was vibrant with the chorus.

Presently a man in a sleeved waistcoat crossed the paddock, whistling lustily, and from somewhere below there rose a merry clatter of plates and dishes; and thus the old inn, which had seen so many mornings, woke up to yet another.

But there never was, there never could be, just such another morning as this was!

And in a little while, having dressed with more than usual care, I went downstairs to find my breakfast awaiting me in the Sanded Parlour, having ordered it for this early hour the night previously—ham and eggs and fragrant coffee, what mortal could wish for more?

And while I ate, waited on by the rosy-cheeked chamber-maid, in came Master Amos Baggett, mine host, to pass the time of day, and likewise to assure me that my baggage should catch the early train; who, when I rose, my meal at an end, paused to wipe his honest hand quite needlessly upon his snowy apron ere he wished me "Good-bye."

So having duly remembered the aforesaid rosy-cheeked chambermaid, the obsequious "Boots," and the grinning ostler, I sallied forth into the sunshine, and crossing the green, where stood the battered sign-post, I came to a flight of rough steps, at the foot of which my boat was moored. In I stepped, cast loose the painter, and shipping the sculls, shot out into the stream.

No, there never was, there never could be, just such another morning as this, for to-day I was to marry Lisbeth, and every stroke of the oar carried me nearer to her and happiness.

Gaily the alders bent and nodded to me; joyfully the birds piped and sang; merrily the water laughed and chattered against my prow as I rowed through the golden morning.

Long before the hour appointed I reached the water-stairs at Fane Court, and, tying my skiff, lighted my pipe and watched the smoke rise slowly into the still air while I tried "to possess my soul in patience."

Sitting thus, I dreamed many a fair dream of the new life that was to be, and made many resolutions, as a man should upon his wedding morn.

And at last came Lisbeth herself, swiftly, lightly, as fair and sweet and fresh as the morning, who yet paused awhile to lean upon the balustrade and look down at me beneath the brim of her hat. Up I rose and stretched out my hands to her, but she still stood there, and I saw her cheeks were flushed and her eyes shy and tender.

So once more we stood upon the old water-stairs, she on the top stair, I on the lower; and again I saw the little foot beneath her skirt come slowly towards me and hesitate.

"Dick," she said, "you know that Aunt Agatha has cut me off—disinherited me altogether—you have had time to think it all over?"

"Yes!"

"And you are quite—quite sure?"

"Quite! I think I have been so all my life."

"I'm penniless now, Dick, a beggar, with nothing in the world but the clothes I wear."

"Yes," I said, catching her hands in mine, "my beggar-maid; the loveliest, noblest, sweetest that ever stooped to bestow her love on man."

"Dick, how glorious everything is this morning—the earth, the sky, and the river!"

"It is our wedding morning!" said I.

"Our wedding day," she repeated in a whisper.

"And there never was just such a morning as this," said I.

"But, Dick, all days cannot be as this—there must be some clouds and storms sometimes, and—and—oh, Dick! are you sure that you will never, never regret——"

"I love you, Lisbeth, in the shadow as well as the sunshine—love you ever and always." And so, the little foot hesitating no longer, Lisbeth came down to me.

Oh, never again could there be such another morning as this!

"Ahoy!"

I looked round with a start, and there, his cap cocked rakishly over one eye, his "murderous cutlass" at his hip and his arms folded across his chest, stood "Scarlet Sam, the Terror of the South Seas."

"Imp!" cried Lisbeth.

"Avast!" cried he in lusty tones; "whereaway?"

I glanced helplessly at Lisbeth and she at me.

"Whereaway, shipmate?" he bellowed in nautical fashion, but before I could find a suitable answer Dorothy made her appearance with the fluffy kitten "Louise" cuddled under her arm as usual.

"How do you do?" she said demurely; "it's awfully nice to get up so early, isn't it? We heard Auntie creeping about on tippity-toes, you know, so we came, too. Reginald said she was pretending to be burglars, but I think she's going 'paddling.' Are you, Auntie?"

"No, dear; not this morning," answered Lisbeth, shaking her head.

"Then you are going for a row in Uncle Dick's boat. How fine!"

"An' you'll take us with you, won't you, Uncle Dick?" cried the Imp eagerly. "We'll be pirates. I'll be 'Scarlet Sam,' an' you can be 'Timothy Bone, the bo'sun,' like you were last time."

"Impossible, my Imp," I said firmly. He looked at me incredulously for a moment, then seeing I meant it, his lip began to quiver.

"I didn't think 'T-Timothy B-Bone' would ever desert me," he said, and turned away.

"Oh, Auntie!" exclaimed Dorothy, "won't you take us?"

"Dear—not this morning."

"Are you going far, then, Uncle Dick?"

"Yes, very far," I answered, glancing uneasily from the Imp's drooping figure to Lisbeth.

"I wonder where?"

"Oh—well—er—down the river," I stammered, quite at a loss.

"Y-e-s, but where?" persisted Dorothy.

"Well, to—er—to——"

"To the 'Land of Heart's Delight,'" Lisbeth put in, "and you may come with us, after all, if Uncle Dick will take you."

"To be sure he will, if your Auntie requires it," I cried, "so step aboard, my hearties, and lively!" In a moment the Imp's hand was in mine, and he was smiling up at me with wet lashes.

"I knew 'Timothy Bone' could never be a—a 'mutinous rogue,'" he said, and turned to aid Dorothy aboard with the air of an admiral on his flagship.

And now, all being ready, he unhitched the painter, or, as he said, "slipped our cable," and we glided out into midstream.

"A ship," he said thoughtfully, "always has a name. What shall we call this one? Last time we were 'pirates' and she was the *Black Death*——"

"Never mind last time, Imp," I broke in; " to-day she is the *Joyful Hope*."

"That doesn't sound very 'pirate-y,' somehow," he responded, with a disparaging shake of the head, "but I s'pose it will have to do."

And so, upon that summer morning, the good ship *Joyful Hope* set sail for the "Land of Heart's Delight," and surely no vessel of her size ever carried quite such a cargo of happiness before or since.

And once again "Scarlet Sam" stamped upon the "quarter-deck" and roared orders anent "lee-shrouds" and "weather braces," with divers injunctions concerning the "helm," while his eyes rolled and he flourished his "murderous cutlass" as he had done upon a certain other memorable occasion.

Never, never again could there be just such another morning as this—for two of us at least.

On we went, past rush and sedge and weeping willow, by roaring weir and cavernous lock, into the shadow of grim stone bridges and out again into the sunshine, past shady woods and green uplands, until at length we "cast anchor" before a flight of steps leading up to a particularly worn stone gateway surmounted by a crumbling stone cross.

"Why," exclaimed the Imp, staring, "this is a church!"

"Imp," I nodded, "I believe it is."

"But to-day isn't Sunday, you know," he remonstrated, seeing it was our intention to land.

"Never mind that, Imp; ' the better the deed, the better the day, you know.'"

On we went, Dorothy and the Imp in front, while Lisbeth and I brought up the rear, and she slipped her hand into mine. In the porch we came upon an aged woman busy with a broom and a very large duster, who, catching sight of us, dropped first the duster and then the broom, and stood staring in open-mouthed astonishment.

And there, in the dim old church, with the morning sun making a glory of the window above our heads, and with the birds for our choristers, the vows were exchanged and the blessing pronounced that gave Lisbeth and her future into my keeping; yet I think we were both conscious of those two small figures in the gloom of the great pew behind, who stared in round-eyed wonderment.

The register duly signed, and all formalities over and done, we go out into the sunshine; and once more the aged woman, richer now by half a crown, is reduced to mute astonishment, so that speech is beyond her when the Imp, lifting his feathered cap, politely wishes her "good morning."

Once more aboard the *Joyful Hope*, there ensued an awkward pause, during which

Lisbeth looked at the children and I at her.

"We must take them back home," she said at last.

"We shall miss our train, Lisbeth."

"But," and here she blushed most delightfully, "there is really no hurry; we can take a—a later one."

"So be it," I said, and laid our course accordingly.

For a time there was silence, during which the Imp, as if in momentary expectation of an attack by bloodthirsty foes, scowled about him, pistol in hand, keeping, as he said, "his weather eye lifting," while Dorothy glanced from Lisbeth to me and back again with puzzled brows.

"I do believe you have been marrying each other!" she said suddenly. The Imp forgot all about his "weather eye" and stared aghast.

"'Course not," he cried at last. "Uncle Dick wouldn't do such a thing, would you, Uncle Dick?"

"Imp, I have—I do confess it."

"Oh!" he exclaimed in a tone of deepest tragedy. "And you let him go and do it, Auntie Lisbeth?"

"He was so very, very persistent, Imp," she said, actually turning crimson beneath his reproachful eye.

"Don't be too hard on us, Imp," I pleaded.

"I s'pose it can't be helped now," he said, a little mollified, but frowning sternly, nevertheless.

"No," I answered, with my eyes upon Lisbeth's blushing face, "it certainly can't be helped now."

"And you'll never do it again?"

"Never again, Imp."

"Then I forgive you, only why—why did you do it?"

"Well, you see, my Imp, I have an old house in the country, a very cosy old place, but it's lonely, horribly lonely, to live by oneself. I've wanted somebody to help me to live in it for a long time, but nobody would, you know, Imp. At last your Auntie Lisbeth has promised to take care of the house and me, to fill the desolate rooms with her voice and sweet presence, and my empty life with her life. You can't quite understand how much this means to me now, Imp, but you will some day, perhaps."

"But are you going to take our Auntie Lisbeth away from us?" cried Dorothy.

"Yes, dear," I answered, "but——"

"Oh, I don't like that one bit!" exclaimed the Imp.

"But you shall come there and stay with us as often as you wish," said Lisbeth.

"That would be perfectly beautiful!" cried Dorothy.

"Yes, but when?" inquired the Imp gloomily.

"Soon," I answered.

"Very soon!" said Lisbeth.

"Will you promise to be 'Timothy Bone, the bo'sun,' an' the 'Black Knight,' an' 'Little-John' whenever I want you to, Uncle Dick?"

"I will, Imp."

"An' make me a long sword with a— a 'deadly point'?"

"Yes," I nodded, "and show you some real ones, too."

"Real ones?" he cried.

"Oh yes, and armour as well; there's lots of it in the old house, you know."

"Let's go now!" he cried, nearly upsetting the boat in his eagerness.

"Oh! Oh, Dick!" cried Lisbeth at this moment, "Dick—there's aunt!"

"Aunt?" I repeated.

"Aunt Agatha, and she sees us; look!"

Turning my head, I beheld a most unexpected sight. Advancing directly upon us was the old boat, that identical weather-beaten tub of a boat in which Lisbeth and I had come so near ending our lives together, the which has already been told in these Chronicles. On the rowing thwart sat Peter, the coachman, and in the stern-sheets, very grim and stiff in the back, her lorgnette to her eyes, was Lady Warburton.

Escape was quite out of the question, and in half a dozen strokes of the oar we were alongside and close under the battery of the lorgnette.

"Elizabeth," she began, in her most ponderous manner, ignoring my presence altogether, "Elizabeth, child, I blush for you."

"Then, aunt, please don't," cried Lisbeth; "I can do quite enough of that for myself. I'm always blushing lately," and as if to prove her words she immediately proceeded to do so.

"Elizabeth," proceeded Lady Warburton, making great play with her lorgnette, "your very shameless, ungrateful letter I received last night. This morning I arose at an objectionably early hour, travelled down in a draughty train, and here I am out on a damp and nasty river in a leaky boat, with my feet horribly wet, but determined to save you from an act which you may repent all your days."

"Excuse me," I said, bowing deeply, "but such heroic devotion cannot be sufficiently appreciated and admired. In Lisbeth's name I beg to thank you; nevertheless——"

"Mr. Brent, I believe?" she said in a tone of faint surprise, as though noticing my presence for the first time.

"At your service, madam!" I answered, with another bow.

"Then I must ask you to convey my ward back to Fane Court immediately; she and the children will accompany me to London at once."

"My dear Lady Warburton," I said, fronting the lorgnette with really admirable fortitude, "it grieves me to deny you this request, but, believe me, it is impossible!"

"Impossible!" she repeated.

"Quite!" I answered. "You here behold the good ship *Joyful Hope*, bound for the 'Land of Heart's Delight,' and we aboard are all determined on our course."

"'An' the wind blows fair an' our helm's a-lee, so it's heave, my mariners, all—O!'" cried the Imp in his nautical voice.

"Dear me!" ejaculated Lady Warburton, staring. "Elizabeth, be so obliging as to tell me what it all means. Why have you dragged these children from their beds to come philandering upon a horrid river at such an hour?"

"Excuse, me, aunt, but she didn't drag us," protested the Imp, bowing exactly as I had done a moment before.

"Oh no, we came," nodded Dorothy.

"An' we've been getting married, you know," said the Imp.

"And it was all very, very beautiful," added Dorothy.

"Married!" cried Lady Warburton in a tone of horror; "married!"

"They would do it, you know," sighed the Imp.

"And quite right, too," said Dorothy; "everybody always marries somebody, some time; it's very fashionable at present. Mamma did, and so shall I when I grow up, I suppose."

"Goodness gracious, child!" exclaimed Lady Warburton.

"I s'pose you're angry 'bout it, aunt," pursued the Imp. "I was at first—just a weeny bit; but you see Uncle Dick has a wonderful house with swords an' armour, but empty, an' he wanted to keep somebody in it to see that everything was nice, I s'pose, an' sing, you know, an' take care of his life. Auntie Lisbeth can sing, an' she wanted to go, so I forgave them."

"Oh, indeed, Reginald?" said Lady Warburton in a rather queer voice, and I saw the corners of her high thin nose quiver strangely.

"Beggin' your pardon, ma'am," said Peter at this moment, touching his cap, "I don't know much about boats, my line bein' 'osses, but I do think as this 'ere boat is a-goin' to sink."

"Then row for the shore instantly," said Lady Warburton firmly, "and should I never reach it alive"—here she brought her lorgnette to bear on Lisbeth—"I say if I *do* meet a watery grave this day, my epitaph shall be, 'Drowned by the Ingratitude of a Niece.'"

However, this gloomy tragedy being happily averted, and Lady Warburton safely landed, I, at a nod from Lisbeth, rowed to the bank likewise, and we all disembarked together.

Now, as kind Fortune would have it, and Fortune was very kind that morning the place where we stood was within a stone's-throw of the Three Jolly Anglers, and wafted to us on the warm, still air there came a wondrous fragrance, far sweeter and more alluring to the hungry than the breath of roses or honeysuckle—the delightful aroma of frying bacon.

Lady Warburton faced us, her parasol tucked beneath her arm, looking very much like a military officer on parade.

"Dorothy and Reginald," she said in a short, sharp voice of command, "bid good-bye to your Auntie Lisbeth and accompany me home at once."

"No, no," cried Lisbeth, with hands stretched out appealingly, "you will not leave us like this, Aunt—for the sake of the love I shall always bear you, and—and——"

"Elizabeth, I cared for you from your babyhood up. Ingratitude is my return. I watched you grow from child to woman. I planned out a future for you; you broke those plans. I might tell you that I am a lonely disappointed old woman, who loved you much more than she thought, but I won't!"

"Dear, dear Aunt Agatha, did you love me so much, and I never guessed; you wouldn't let me, you see. Ah! do not think me ungrateful, but when a woman comes to marry she must choose for herself, as I have done; and I am happy, dear, and proud of my choice—proud to have won the true love of a true man; only do not think I am ungrateful. And if this must be good-bye, do not let us part like this—for my sake and your sake and the sake of my—husband."

Lady Warburton had turned away, and there ensued a somewhat embarrassing pause.

"Elizabeth," she said suddenly, "if I don't mistake, somebody is frying bacon somewhere, and I'm ravenously hungry."

"So am I," cried the Imp.

"And so am I," Dorothy chimed in.

"Then suppose we have breakfast," I suggested, and in almost less time than it takes to tell I was leading the way across the green with Lady Warburton on my arm—actually leaning on my arm.

And now who so surprised to see us as honest Amos Baggett, ushering us with many bows and smiles into the Sanded Parlour, where breakfast was soon ready; and who so quick and dexterous in attending to our wants as the rosy-cheeked chambermaid?

And what a breakfast that was! Never had the antique andirons on the hearth, the pewter plates and dishes upon the walls, the brass-bound blunderbuss above the mantel, seemed so bright and polished before, and surely never had they gleamed upon a merrier company. To be sure, the Imp's remarks were somewhat few and far between, but that was simply on account of the blackberry jam.

"I suppose you are both ridiculously happy," said Lady Warburton, eyeing us over her coffee-cup.

"Most absurdly!" answered Lisbeth, blushing all in a moment.

"Preposterously!" I nodded.

"Of course!" said Lady Warburton, and setting down her cup, she sighed, while I wondered what memories her narrow life could hold.

"Uncle Dick," said the Imp suddenly,

"do you s'pose Scarlet Sam ever ate black-berry jam?"

"Undoubtedly, my Imp, when he could get it." This appeared greatly to relieve his mind, for he took another helping.

But all things must have an end, alas!—even such a breakfast as this, and presently we were out in the sunshine again, standing beneath the weather-beaten sign whereon three faded fishermen fished with faded rods in a faded stream; while away down the road we could see Peter already approaching with the carriage.

"And now I suppose you are going?" said Lady Warburton.

"There is a train at half-past ten," I answered.

"An' we are going too!" said Dorothy.

"Yes, we're quite ready, Uncle Dick!" cried the Imp, thrusting his pistols into his belt.

"But you wouldn't leave me all alone, would you, children?" asked Lady War-burton, and there was a certain wistfulness in her sharp face that seemed new to it.

"'Course not," sighed the Imp, "only——"

"We must stay and take care of her, Reginald," nodded Dorothy decisively.

"Yes, I'll take care of you, Aunt, with lance, battle-axe, an' sword, by day an' night," said the Imp, "only—I should have liked to see Uncle Dick's wonderful house, with the real swords an' armour, in the Land of Heart's Delight—some day, you know."

"And so you shall!" cried Lady Warburton, and she actually stooped to kiss him, and then Dorothy, rather "pecky" kisses, perhaps, but very genuine kisses notwithstanding.

"Richard," she said, giving me her hand, "we shall come down to your wonderful house—all three of us, next week, so be prepared—now be off—both of you."

"Then you forgive me, Aunt?" asked Lisbeth, hesitating.

"Well, I don't quite know yet, Lisbeth, but, my dear, I'll tell you something I have never mentioned to a living soul but you if I had acted forty years ago as you did to-day, I should have been a very different creature from the cross-grained old woman you think me. There—there's a kiss, but as for forgiving you—that is quite another matter, I must have time to think it over. Good-bye, my dear and, Richard, fill her life with happiness, to make up for mine, if you can. Children, bid good-bye to your Auntie—and Uncle Dick!"

"You won't forget the sword with the deadly point,' will you, Uncle Dick?"

"I won't forget, my Imp!" Hereupon he tried to smile, but his trembling lips refused, and snatching his hand from mine, he turned away; as for Dorothy, she was sobbing into the fur of the fluffy kitten

Then I helped Lisbeth aboard the *Joyful Hope*, loving her the more for the tears that gleamed beneath her long lashes, and "casting loose," we glided out into the stream.

There they stood, the two children, with the white-haired figure between them, Dorothy holding up the round-eyed "Louise," for a parting glimpse, and the Imp flourishing his cutlass, until a bend of the river hid them from view.

So Lisbeth and I sailed on together through the golden morning to the "Land of Heart's Delight."